"Do I understand yo   **S0-ASY-118** sider giving me a child if we were married and I courted you?" Bill asked.

Katie sat back in her chair. "Put the other way around—courtship first, marriage second—possibly. I refuse to be cheated out of a courtship."

He frowned. "How long?"

"I'm not sure—a lot depends on whether I like you."

"You already like me."

"Not the new you. But here's the condition: You must complete your end of the bargain first—before I promise anything," she said.

"What? Are you out of your mind? How do I know I can trust you?"

"You yourself said we've always been the best of friends. If I didn't lie to you or cheat you when we were kids, you know I won't now. Waiting gives us a chance to renew our friendship, puts us on a safe footing."

He thought for a few moments, then rose abruptly and stalked over to her end of the table. Katie saw the fiery glow in his eyes, heard his soft laughter. His fingers stroked her neck, then tangled in her hair. "What—what are you doing?" she asked.

He pulled her out of the chair, hauling her to him. "Sealing the bargain." He kissed her eyes, her cheeks. "I accept your terms, Katie." He nipped the side of her chin. "All of them." His hands slid down her spine. "Your rules, courtship, marriage, the works." He drew her even closer to him. "Kiss me, Katie," he demanded. "Kiss me. . . ."

## WHAT ARE *LOVESWEPT* ROMANCES?

They are stories of true romance and touching emotion. We believe those two very important ingredients are constants in our highly sensual and very believable stories in the *LOVESWEPT* line. Our goal is to give you, the reader, stories of consistently high quality that may sometimes make you laugh, sometimes make you cry, but are always fresh and creative and contain many delightful surprises within their pages.

Most romance fans read an enormous number of books. Those they truly love, they keep. Others may be traded with friends and soon forgotten. We hope that each *LOVESWEPT* romance will be a treasure—a "keeper." We will always try to publish

*LOVE STORIES YOU'LL NEVER FORGET*
*BY AUTHORS YOU'LL ALWAYS REMEMBER*

The Editors

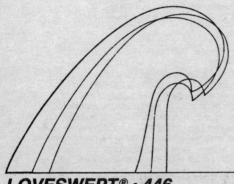

**LOVESWEPT® • 446**

# Doris Parmett
# Sweet Mischief

 BANTAM BOOKS
NEW YORK • TORONTO • LONDON • SYDNEY • AUCKLAND

SWEET MISCHIEF

*A Bantam Book / January 1991*

*If you would be interested in receiving protective vinyl
covers for your Loveswept books, please write to this
address for information:*

> *Loveswept*
> *Bantam Books*
> *P. O. Box 985*
> *Hicksville, NY 11802*

ISBN 0-553-44082-9

*Published simultaneously in the United States and Canada*

# One

"Sweet Mischief, delectable edibles. How may I help you?" Katie Reynolds chirped her standard greeting into the phone.

While waiting for an answer, she cradled the handset between her chin and shoulder, freeing both hands. Long accustomed to doing more than one thing at a time, she scribbled her signature at the bottom of a purchase order, then flipped through a pile of letters. Failing to get an immediate response from the caller, she repeated her greeting.

"I call your offer mighty tempting," a masculine voice said. "Are you one?"

"One what?" she asked distractedly, dismayed by the huge bill for new carpeting. She'd ordered it to replace the almost new carpet that had been ruined a month earlier when a water pipe had burst during the night, flooding her chocolate shop.

"A delectable edible," the man stated.

Katie snapped to attention. Her feet hit the floor. Not again! she thought. She'd like to get her hands on the jerk who had been pestering her for the last several weeks and wring his neck! Crank callers were sickos. She didn't need him tying up her line, possibly ruining a phone sale. She had considered changing the store's phone number, but had opted for waiting a while longer, hoping the crank caller would tire of his game. If she changed the number, she'd have the expense of notifying customers and printing new stationery and labels for the gift boxes.

She glanced at the wall clock. Usually the fool contented himself with heavy breathing, and phoned nearer closing time, not lunchtime.

Katie kept her tone casual. "Mister, let's clear the line and still be friends."

"No thanks. I'd prefer seeing for myself if you're a delectable edible."

Roiling anger ended all pretense at playing it cool. "Fine," she snapped. "Suppose you send me a picture of yourself. If your hair is steel-blue, your eyes gun-metal purple, and your face green, I'll consider it. If not, bug off!"

A roar of laughter assailed her ear, then a cheery voice said, "You haven't changed a bit, have you, Red? You're still the same sassy-mouthed brat. How are you?"

Her fury skidded to a halt. Her hand froze in midair. Her pulse quickened. Only one person dared call her "Red." Katie mentally flipped through the pictures of her high-school sophomore yearbook. Closing her eyes, she brought one special face into mental focus. Ink-black hair flopped carelessly over his forehead, almost obscuring his straight black eyebrows. Midnight-blue eyes twinkled teasingly. A wide grin split his full lips. Chiseled classical features and a strong jaw added character to his face.

"Keep talking," she ordered, wanting to make certain her vital organs were creating turmoil over the right man.

A chuckle, more of a familiar rumble, rolled over the phone wires, erasing the years. "Brat, are you still getting into trouble? Is that why you've named your store Sweet Mischief?"

"Bill, you devil!" Katie bounced off her chair, sending letters scattering onto the floor. "You're back. The phantom's returned! I can't believe it! What are you doing here? Is this another one of those fast sorry-I-don't-have-time-to-see-you business trips that brought you here last time?"

"I phoned you. It's not my fault you're so popular that you weren't home. Do I get any points for having written?"

She scoffed. "Four letters after your college graduation do not qualify you for a good conduct medal. But since I've been too busy to write you myself these last few years, I forgive you. Enough recriminations. Where are you *this* minute?"

He named a posh hotel on Beach Avenue. "I'm sorry that I don't have steel-blue hair or purple eyes and a green face, but I'd love to take you and your husband to dinner tonight, if you're free."

Katie's bubble of excitement deflated. She wilted against her desk. Naturally he'd expect a woman of thirty to be married, as many of her friends were, including her store manager, Phyllis Newton. Phyllis, seven months pregnant, kept urging her to find a man, and accused her of being married to the store. Katie supposed it was true. Since she had taken over Sweet Mischief several years earlier, she had avoided any serious commitments and had even turned down one offer of marriage. She preferred devoting her time to the store, trying to make it a comfortably profitable business.

She forced herself to answer Bill with studied ease. "I'm single. I've set my sights on other goals. When Aunt Agnes died, I inherited her candy store. I renamed it Sweet Mischief and have been working hard at upgrading its image. It's satisfying work, but it can be all-consuming. So tell me, how are your parents?"

"Fine. Dad retired a couple of years ago. Mom's taken up golf to play with him. They live the good life in Palm Springs. They're still each other's best friends."

She recalled his parents with fondness, and remembered her sadness when they moved to California during Bill's freshman year in college. Mr. Logan had had an offer to join his brother's construction firm. For a few years the families had exchanged Christmas cards, but eventually the ties had slipped away.

"Say," Bill said, "do you remember the last time we cut school to go surfing?"

"Absolutely." What a day! she thought. With the sun at his back, his eyes matching sapphires, Bill had resembled a tall, tanned pirate, gliding atop the waves on his board as if born to the sea.

"You bet me you'd win," she said. "You did too, you louse. The pizza and you ate up my money!"

"I often think of those carefree days," he said, "days when you trailed after me. Do you, Katie?"

Perhaps it was his tone, the evocative implication of how much they had shared, but familiar longing washed over her. Yes, she remembered. Far too much. Far too often. Mostly about her prayers that Bill would see her as a woman, not his childhood buddy, two years his junior.

"Of course I think about those 'good old days,' " she said, deriving a measure of pleasure that he remembered. "You used starvation as a standard excuse to steal my lunch."

He chuckled. "Trust you, Katie, to have a perfect memory. What are you doing for dinner tonight?"

She pictured herself heating up a frozen chicken dinner, eating it on a tray table before the television set. "Aside from a dinner engagement with the president, nothing."

"Break it. I'll pick you up at the house at eight. Please. Okay?"

For years she had carefully hidden her love for Bill behind the guise of friendship. After a ponderous silence, during which she imagined herself enviously seated across from him and his wife, she said, "All right. I'd love to have dinner with and your wife."

"I'm alone this trip, Katie."

*Oh!* She mouthed the word, fevered with curiosity. Removing her glasses, she pinched the bridge of her nose, then caught her normally unconscious habit. The last time she had seen Bill, she hadn't needed to wear glasses. At least she knew her figure was attractive. Bicycle riding and long walks helped maintain a svelte shape. Still, what would Bill think seeing her now, no longer a fresh-faced, wrinkle-free teenager?

She listened to the disastrous knocking of her heart and knew she'd risk anything to see him again.

"Until later, Katie."

"Until later, Bill."

The line clicked, ending further discussion. For a long moment Katie waited for her breathing to even. What was going on? she wondered. What was going on, her conscience answered her, was that she was reading more into a casual dinner between two old friends than was healthy or wise.

"Definitely," she muttered.

Oh, no! she thought suddenly. The house! Bill was going to see how run-down it had become. Thanks to her plowing every spare penny into Sweet Mischief, her house was slowly changing from an elegant turn-of-the-century Victorian to an expensive-to-fix white elephant. While she adored her home's high-ceilinged rooms and oak floors, the gingerbread and lattice exterior, she lived with peeling paint and chipped plaster, a back porch that sloped precariously, a driveway buckled by tree roots, and a myriad of big and little items she'd lived with so long, she'd become oblivious to them.

Much as she longed to restore her home to its former shining beauty, she lacked one essential ingredient. Money. She understood why, to make ends meet, many owners converted their lovely Victorian homes into bed-and-breakfast inns.

Still, despite her financial straits, Katie wouldn't live anywhere else. She loved Cape May. Named in the 1600s for Dutch Captain Cornelius Jacobsen Mey, Cape May had served as a summer refuge for five United States presidents. She loved the one-hundred-year-old shade trees that lined its streets, the masses of tulips honoring its Dutch heritage, the over six hundred late nineteenth-century frame structures that drew tourists from all over the world to glimpse this fascinating heritage of the Victorian era. Located at the southern tip of New Jersey, one hundred and fifty miles south of New York City, Cape May County juts out between the Atlantic Ocean and Delaware Bay.

Gazing around her office, Katie inhaled deeply, savoring the aroma of chocolate wafting through the open door to the shop. The small office doubled as an additional storage area. Gold foil boxes, embellished with Sweet Mischief's seashell logo, were stacked in neat columns along the wall opposite her second-hand desk and chair. A gooseneck lamp, recycled from the attic, plus two metal file cabinets donated by friends completed the unimpressive decor. But it was all hers, and she was fiercely proud of it.

Katie's independent streak had been obvious from her birth. The only child of an older couple, into whose life Katie stunningly appeared when her mother was forty-one and her father fifty, she soon overwhelmed her parents, growing from infancy to toddler to preschooler with boundless energy. The day she started kindergarten had been a joyous one for all.

Bill Logan lived down the block from the Reynolds. Once she discovered a possible playmate, she dogged his footsteps. She learned to play the games he played. Bill good-naturedly took his "shadow" in stride. He filled for her the roles of brother, confidant, tutor, and co-conspirator. But never boyfriend.

With some embarrassment, Katie remembered one rainy Sunday morning, when she, a thirteen-year-old wearing a training bra, sat in the pew directly behind fifteen-year-old Bill, fidgeting. For months she had wrestled with bouts of dissatisfaction. Nameless, shapeless dissatisfaction.

From her gym teacher, and not her mother, she had learned to recognize her mood swings as part of growing up. "Hormones," the teacher had explained, pointing to a growth chart. Bodily changes.

The knowledge didn't make living through them easier. For the first time in her memory, she refrained from sharing her intensely private feelings with Bill, whose voice had deepened. He shaved and splashed cologne on his face.

Just the previous evening she had accused him of wearing perfume. He'd swatted her bottom, then whistled down her path on his way to a date. Her girlfriends envied her friendship with him.

"Tell him about us," they begged. "You're his buddy, Katie." They frankly discussed what they'd like to do with him, and what they'd like him to do to them.

Their suggestions raced through Katie's mind that Sunday. Instead of listening to the minister, she concentrated on the fine shape of Bill's head, his perfect ears, and the way his dark hair curled over his white shirt collar. She mentally measured the width of his broad shoulders, comparing him to the other boys. Her squirming must have made a noise. Suddenly he turned, wagging his finger as if to say, "Naughty, naughty."

Mortified, she stuck out her tongue, trimmed up her chin, and buried her face in her hymnal, the words swimming before her eyes. Gradually she willed her cheeks to pale, her stomach to settle. She wiped the palms of her hands, chastising herself for giving Bill's gesture importance. She returned to her daydreams. In her mind's eye she saw his lean body in a bathing suit, his powerful legs churning, his muscular arms breaking the water as he raced the length of the pool in a burst of speed. Then he hoisted himself out and, with water streaming down his bare chest and legs, walked toward her, one hand outstretched. . . .

Katie was still lost in her reverie when Phyllis entered the office. She settled her ample girth in a chair, adjusting to a comfortable position. Her skin shone with the special glow of impending motherhood. "Here's the mock-up of the new ad," she said, holding up a piece of paper. "How do you like it?"

"It's wonderful," Katie replied dreamily.

"You might try looking at it first." Phyllis waved the paper beneath Katie's nose.

She pushed it away and focused on her friend. "You'll never guess who called me."

"Judging from the expression on your face, I'd say you won the Publisher's Clearing House Giveaway. Lend me a thou, would you?"

"Bill's back."

Phyllis sucked in her breath. "And?"

Katie smiled. "He asked me to have dinner with him tonight."

Phyllis scowled. "And?"

"I know what you're thinking, Phil—"

"I wish you did," Phyllis said sharply. "You've

always had romantic notions where he's concerned. Face it, Katie. Bill never dated you. He knew you too well. You held no mystery for him. Remember how you complained that he treated you like his kid sister at Janice Mortman's party?"

"So?" Katie asked.

"So learn."

Katie sighed, once more catapulting back into her memories. Fifteen then, she'd spent hours primping for Janice's party. Ever popular with the boys, Janice had received a jukebox from her parents for her birthday. That made her even more popular. Halfway through the evening, Bill had danced one obligatory dance with Katie. As the last chords of the song blasted around them, Katie, anxious to know what he thought of her appearance, had asked, "Well, what do you think?"

Completely missing her point, Bill had glanced around the room. "I think Janice Mortman is gorgeous. See you later, squirt."

Feeling like an old shoe, Katie had watched Bill dance with Janice, holding her so close that Katie couldn't tell where one left off and the other began. Starting that night Bill went steady with Janice, who bragged about her conquest to all the girls. Several months later Bill and Janice broke up. One day Bill arrived on Katie's doorstep, hauled her outside, and sternly lectured her on why some men couldn't be trusted.

"Men like you?" she'd asked teasingly.

"Especially like me!" he had barked.

Katie gave herself a hard, mental shake. "Phyllis, Janice's party was a long time ago."

"Honey, I'm your friend. You cried on my shoulder when Bill's letters dwindled after those first few years. Pardon me if I'm not as thrilled as you. Knowing you, Katie, if he makes one move toward you, you'll let him break your heart. He'll leave again, then what? More heartache?"

Katie lifted her chin in a defiant gesture. "All I'm doing is going out to dinner with him. I'm not marrying the man! You're unfair. You don't know what he's like now." She ran a trembling hand over her hair. Trying out a new hairstyle that morning, she'd worn it in a sleek French braid.

"Is he married?"

Katie stared at the wall rather than risk Phyllis's censure. "How should I know?"

"You didn't ask?"

She hesitated. "No, I didn't. I assume he is."

Phyllis slapped her knee. "Deliver me from people who refuse to learn. Don't say I didn't warn you."

"How do you know so much?" Katie asked crossly.

"Let's say I believe in caution. Go to dinner if you must. Ask about his wife and kiddies, then forget him. If not, you're begging for trouble. I've no doubt Bill's a good-looking man. You'll be tempted. His being here alone makes the situation pure dynamite."

"For goodness' sake," Katie protested, "you sound as if I'm incapable of spending an evening with him without falling into his bed."

"You've got enough troubles trying to keep this place afloat."

"Oh, quit worrying," Katie muttered, not believing a word she said. As Phyllis started to leave, she handed her the ad. "It's a good one. We'll run it."

Katie knew that Phyllis's advice was well intentioned. When they were still teenagers she had embellished the stories of her dates to keep Bill from guessing the truth. Her love for him intensified, although he continued treating her in his usual brotherly fashion. He protected her, teased her, and dragged her to the beach for serious swimming practice. Both excelled at water sports: Bill, the more powerful swimmer; Katie, the more graceful diver. They starred on the school's swim team. From her perch high above the Olympic-size pool, she would lift up and off the board, her senses heightened by Bill's watchful presence. She would cut through the water with the keenness of a newly sharpened blade, then surface, eagerly seeking his approval.

If the past were prologue, tonight she'd hide her feelings. She'd be polite, show interest in his work, and send him home with regards to his parents and a family that by now probably included a wife and children.

Bill Logan hung up the phone. His smile faded, replaced by a thoughtful look. On the bed lay his custom-tailored suit jacket. From the inside pocket he retrieved a report detailing Katie's bleak financial status. He had learned in confidence that her huge old house needed repairs. He knew about the broken water main in her shop, and that she had mortgaged her home to the hilt to pay for the damages. Without an infusion of capital—at least a seventy-five percent increase in sales—she risked a better than even chance of going broke within the year. Unless . . . unless

Katie agreed to his eminently fair business proposition.

He stretched out on the bed and folded his hands behind his head. Katie held the key, the solution to his problem—and to hers. True, his business proposal might shock her at first, but he was confident he could convince her of the wisdom of saying yes. He'd point out the advantages. Who knew her better than he?

Over the last few years he'd come to realize his life needed a meaningful purpose, a new direction. No longer did the party scene interest him. What he wanted was a son. But he wan't prepared to attain his goal by marrying and living through the miseries he'd seen his friends endure, especially the devastating divorce his friend Gil had gone through recently with his wife Nancy. He'd never seen such hostility in people who had once loved each other. And the nonsense they fought over. Linens, garden furniture, and designer shower curtains!

Friendship, the kind he had always enjoyed with Katie, guaranteed a nice, uncomplicated relationship. Not being in love, not wanting to marry, freed him to decide his future sensibly.

He knew Katie liked children. Actually, he knew everything about his Katie. Quite a comforting thought. Too bad the many women he had dated over the past decade hadn't possessed Katie's qualities. She was blessed with an agile mind, a quick wit, a sense of humor, but mostly he liked her agreeable nature. To be fair, the women he dated harbored one or two of Katie's favorable attributes, but as he had dispassionately considered each woman's candidacy, Katie continued to rise to the forefront as the logical choice to be the mother of his son. Upon reflection, he realized the reason was simple.

He liked her!

Grinning, Bill congratulated himself on his brainstorm and the good fortune of his timing. Unfortunately for her—and providentially for him—she was nearly broke. This month of December was looking especially bleak for her. Cape May's thriving summer business fell off in winter as vacationers sought warmer climes. Yes, Katie needed his protection, just as she had always needed it. He smiled, remembering how he'd warned more than one of her boyfriends to keep his hands to himself or answer to him.

He would turn Katie's misfortune into fortune for them both. He'd gladly assume her debts and restore her house to its original charm. He'd see to it she'd be financially independent. She'd live in luxury.

They both hailed from hard-working, middle-class families, and he knew Katie had always assumed the chances were good she'd marry and have children. Traditional families were in the minority now, though. Certainly from a practical standpoint, his solution made perfect sense. Why shouldn't single men and women have children? Single-parent households were on the increase. He knew his Katie. She had always followed him around like a puppy, seeking his approval. He'd been well aware of her soft spot for him. There-fore, there was a residue of good feeling. He'd cap-italize on it that night. Offering to have her husband join them for dinner had been a ploy to find out if she had met a special man within the last month. Apparently she hadn't. He didn't dwell on why that pleased him so much, but continued mentally outlining his plan.

He would return to California, but naturally he'd visit Katie monthly for the duration of her pregnancy to check on her health and progress. To keep her company during his absence, he'd buy her a nice, large guard dog. Although his personal preference was to own a Saint Bernard, if Katie wanted a police dog or an Irish setter, he'd get her one.

After the birth of his son, he'd return to Cape May, buy a house—near Katie's for his son's sake—and open an office. Given the nature of his restoration business, it didn't matter where he headquartered.

His plan formed the cornerstone of his future. He'd give Katie anything she desired as long as she understood theirs was a business arrangement and she didn't fawn all over him. With her agreeable personality, the odds were she'd be overwhelmed with gratitude. The thought gave him pause, then he decided he could deal with that problem too. Fully aware of her buoyant, enthusiastic nature, he'd simply tamp down her appreciation when he presented his plan to restore her house and save Sweet Mischief.

Reassured by his assessment, he undressed to shower and shave. His body was still lean and hard, maintained by working out in his private gym and swimming laps in his pool. Humming, he strode confidently into the bathroom. He smiled at his reflection, showing a row of gleaming white teeth, and ran his fingers through his thick black hair. Tonight it was crucial that he be at his charming best. After all, it wasn't every day he asked a woman to have his baby.

# Two

Katie kept a tenuous grip on her nerves and a cautious eye on the clock as she coaxed her car's ailing motor to turn over. Home at last by six-thirty, she quickly vacuumed the parlor's thread-bare carpet, then positioned a chair on either side of the dining room pocket doors to hide the broken hinges.

"Hors d'oeuvres!" She flew into the kitchen, opening and closing cabinets on a hunt. The easiest appetizer she knew how to make was tuna pâté. She blended it, then scooped the contents into a bowl and added horseradish and a dash of table smoke for flavor. She put the pâté on a platter, garnished it with parsley sprigs, circled the dish with a ring of crackers, then scurried upstairs.

After showering, she brushed her hair until it shone and, rather than go to the trouble of braiding it again, let it hang about her shoulders. She inserted her new contact lenses with a minimum of difficulty. Makeup in place, she changed into a basic black dress, cinching it at the waist with a black belt. She slipped on a strand of faux pearls and completed her attire with pearl earrings.

"It's as good as it gets," she muttered, dabbing perfume behind her ears and on her wrists.

At precisely eight o'clock Bill rang the doorbell. Excitement rippled through her as she whizzed out of the room and down the flight of stairs. Unfortunately, she forgot the warped step groove at the base. She caught her heel, hitting the floor with a thud.

"Oh, noooo!"

Looking through the glass door, Bill witnessed her fall. "Katie!" he yelled, seeing her clutch her leg. "I'm breaking down the door. Don't move!"

"No, don't do that!" she shouted. "The door's unlocked. I'm all right."

He rushed inside. Katie, her hair tumbling about her face, lay sprawled on the floor, her dress hiked up to her thighs, cursing. One ripped stocking displayed her knee. Her necklace had broken, scattering pearls in different directions. Her hand flew to her right eye.

"Watch out," she warned, scrambling onto her knees. "I've lost a contact lens." She glanced up. "Hi."

He shook his head at her. It wasn't the grand reunion he'd planned. "Hello to you too. When did you start wearing glasses?" He palmed the floor, helping look for the missing lens.

She concentrated on the search, self-conscious over her predicament. "A few years ago. If I could see you, I'd compliment you on your looks. This isn't my usual greeting, Bill. I was going to shake your hand and offer you a drink."

He let his gaze roam appreciatively over her slender figure, the curve of her thigh, her rounded bottom. "The drink can wait. I wasn't going to shake your hand. Old friends deserve something more than a handshake. Did you hurt yourself?"

She forced a smile. "Only my pride. As you can see, the house has gotten a lot older since you saw it last."

Bill hid his own smile. He had surveyed the exterior of the house, the fish-scale shingled roof, the balustrade, the wraparound porch. All needed immediate replacement. He was delighted by his good fortune.

Finding the lens, he curled his fingers over her palm. "Don't drop it. Up you go." To her pleasurable surprise, he carried her up the stairs. "I thought you'd like to change your stockings."

As he mounted the stairs with his feather-light burden, the idea of their conceiving a son in this venerable old beauty of a home pleased him enormously.

"I've moved into my parents' old room," she told him. "I've always loved the belvedere, especially at night. When I was younger I used to stand on the pavilion and make up stories about the people on board the ocean liners."

He crossed the room and opened the door to the belvedere. As he stepped out into the cool night air, still holding her in his arms, he made a mental note to reinforce and paint the belvedere. A breeze tousled her hair, tickling a curl against his neck. He smiled down at her. Would his son be red-haired like his mother, or dark-haired like his father? With her help, she would bring renewed purpose into his life.

"Look Katie, there's the north star. Make a wish."

Wishes were dangerous, Katie thought, staring up at him. She laughed, purposely keeping it light. "You mean, if I say abracadabra the hard-wood floors in my bedroom will miraculously be refinished, or the cheval mirror will be refaced?"

His voice was a husky sound in her ear. "I've learned one thing in life. Given the right circumstances, wishes do come true."

A knot of tension tightened in her breast as she surrendered herself to the exquisite joy of Bill holding her. She had dreamed of this. With her head nestled on his muscular chest, she listened to his strong heartbeat, breathed in his manly scent, and gave thanks for her little accident. When he finally put her down, their thighs aligned for a brief, intimate moment. Flustered, she dashed into the bathroom to repair the damage.

Safe behind a closed door, she pressed her hands to her hot face. She'd thought it would be so easy seeing him again. But who was she fooling? His touch had been enough to send her soaring. She examined her reflection in the mirror. How could she feel so different and look the same? Then she remembered Phyllis's warning and lectured herself as she changed her stockings.

"There, that's better," she said as she joined him in the dining room. "Nothing like a grand entrance, is there?"

He smiled at her with such gentleness, she blushed. "At least it was memorable. All of it." He handed her a flute of wine. "It's good to be back. A toast, Katie. To yesteryear and tomorrow. May it bring each of us our dream."

"And what is yours?" she asked, looking away to pass him the platter of pâté and crackers. The mature Bill radiated more sex appeal than she remembered in the teenager. Her heart was doing a little dance, and she took a quick calming breath.

He sipped his wine. "We'll get to me later. Let's talk about you. Tell me what you've been up to? How's the store coming along?"

"I love it, although it is a lot of work. But it's given me a terrific opportunity to utilize the marketing training I received in college. Right now I'm working on ways to boost my income."

"What have you thought about doing?"

She leaned forward. "I'm investigating the mail-order business. It should help pick up the slack. I don't want to go into the supply end of the business."

"Why?" he asked.

She shrugged. "Primarily because it doesn't interest me. Also I'd need larger quarters, more equipment, and trained help. Mail-order requires less capital outlay. There's a supplier I know who'll give me a better break on the wholesale prices."

"It sounds sensible," he said, admiring her acumen. They should do quite well when it came to their negotiations.

"And then there's this house," she added, blithely increasing his confidence. "One of these days the Historical Society will get after me, demanding I spruce up the place. There are times when I think owning a registered landmark is more a pain than a pleasure."

"Do you want to sell?" he asked, raising his voice over the racket made by the heating pipes.

"No. I love the old place. When my parents moved, I convinced them to let me buy it. I hate the thought of strangers living here. I'll make it work."

"I admire your tenacity, but then you always were a scrapper."

Hiding a frown, she slathered pâté on a cracker. "Scrapper" was not the best compliment she'd ever received.

"Tell me about you, Bill."

"My work keeps me pretty busy. As you know, after I graduated from college I went to work for my uncle. He specializes in landmark and building restorations. I love the work, especially having lived in Cape May. I enjoyed working alongside my dad too. A few years ago I was promoted to manager, and I traveled to various sites. Uncle John's retired, so now I'm president of the company."

Bill wandered over to the window, briefly noting the chipped weatherboard. "Katie," he asked over his shoulder, "do you still swim?"

"Not often. Why? Do I look out of condition?"

He came back to the table. She looked anything but out of condition. He admired her perfect, childbearing hips, the proud thrust of her breasts. "Not at all. It's important to take good physical care of yourself."

"Bill, what's gotten into you? I've never known you to speak in riddles."

"You're quite right." He eyed the chandelier's brittle wiring. "I may be able to help you restore this place. Do you mind if I take a quick tour?"

Katie squinted at him. She did not feel like touring her home. What kind of a reunion was this? "Go ahead. It's a remodeler's paradise."

He was gone for nearly ten minutes, during which time Katie devoured six pâté-covered crackers and wondered what was wrong with Bill. She may not have seen him for several years, but he seemed oddly on edge.

"You're right," he said jubilantly when he returned. "It's falling down around you."

"Thanks," she said dryly. "Bill, change the subject. Suppose you tell me your dream."

He had considered waiting until they'd returned from the restaurant, but with the musical pipes, the snowflakes of plaster, the warped floor in the foyer, now seemed as good a time as any.

"My dream is as old as time."

"That old?" she teased, blushing under his intense gaze. "What is it?"

"A son. I'd like a son before I'm too old to enjoy him."

Katie almost choked on her wine. She'd completely forgotten about his wife. "Is your wife pregnant? Are we toasting impending fatherhood?"

He looked surprised. "Where did you get the idea I'm married? I told you I'm alone."

She quelled a sense of euphoria. "Maybe the fall

messed up my hearing. You're drinking a toast to fatherhood, yet you're unmarried?"

He grinned, dazzling her with his smile. "To the best of my knowledge, none of the women I've dated is pregnant. I'm aware of my social responsibilties."

"Are you getting engaged?" she asked cautiously. Why be ecstatic for nothing?

"No."

"So what we're doing is toasting a hypothetical situation."

"One that I intend to change, yes."

"Good luck," she said glumly.

"Good luck to us both." He saluted her with his glass. "Let's return to your problems for a minute. I can help if you'd let me. What are good friends for?"

She looked at him gloomily. The conversation had gotten off track. "The quickest way to lose a friend is by accepting charity, which I wouldn't. I have a feeling your price is out of my range."

"It won't be charity, Katie." He took both her hands in his. "I have an idea . . ."


For nearly a minute her vocal chords were in shock. *"Whaaat?"* she exclaimed the second they recovered. "You want me to have your baby!"

"Son," he repeated.

"Are you crazy?"

Bill hadn't expected her reaction to be quite so explosive. He'd counted on a residue of friendship to overcome her initial awkwardness. Then they would discuss his more than fair solution like two adults. He removed the pâté knife from her clenched fingers.

"It's really quite sensible," he said hurriedly. "Each of us wants something. Neither of us is getting younger. We'd be helping each other."

She stared at him as if he'd lost his mind. "You're mad."

"No, I'm not. Just hear me out. For goodness' sake don't aim that glass at me!"

"Bill, are you in love with me?"

"Of course not. I haven't seen you in years, but I've always remembered you with the greatest fondness."

"I rest my case. Trust me, you're totally bonkers."

"Knock it off, Katie. This is me. Love had nothing to do with this. Friendship is more important than love. Consider the divorce rate. Half of all marriages end with the husband and wife hating each other, fighting over possessions, making lawyers rich. They pull the poor kids in two directions. At least I'm honest. Can you truly admit you've never thought about wanting a child?"

"Most women do," she said flatly.

"There, you see. If you think about it, my suggestion makes perfect sense."

Katie swilled the rest of her wine. "Then you wear the maternity clothes!"

His glaze slid to her stomach. "Now who's not making sense?"

"Bill, I swear you've lost your mind. You waltz back into my life with a preposterous suggestion that I should have your baby—pardon me, your son!—in return for paying my debts. Are you on some sort of drug?"

He stiffened. "Katie, you know me better than that."

She refilled her glass, swigged the contents, and threw up her hands. "Do I? Do you honestly expect me to trade nine months of my life to fix a leaky roof? Why don't you find a woman, fall in love, do it the old-fashioned way? You know—first comes love, then comes marriage, then comes baby in the baby carriage."

A self-derisive smile twisted his mouth. "I don't seem to stay in love beyond the infatuation stage. What about you? Have you been in love?"

She reared back. "That's none of your business."

"Katie, when you were a kid you told me all your dreams. Those dreams included wanting a large family. I'm only asking for one small son. That's why I came back. I thought if you're not married and not going with anyone, I would tell you my idea. Naturally I wouldn't expect something for nothing. So what if we're not in love? Put down that knife! Think of all the children who are conceived in love, and then the parents divorce in hate. My way is better."

Katie heard alarm systems going off in her head. She wasn't a drinking woman, but at the moment she felt as if she could put away a fifth. As a teenager she would have died to get Bill to pay attention to her. Now, for all the wrong reasons, he'd offered her the most intimate attention. Dressed impeccably in a dark blue suit, blue shirt, and matching tie, he looked serene, successful, and sure of himself.

Either he was a blithering idiot, or she was. "Bill, you're an idiot. I think you'd better leave."

He fastened his gaze on her. "Dammit, Katie, calm down. Granted the conditions aren't typical, but they're not atypical either. Couples set their own standards today. What's so terrible about my wanting a son? At least I want him for the right reasons. I'm a wealthy man and I love children. I just don't happen to be in love, nor do I want to get married. Since when is it a crime? I'm offering you and our son a secure future."

"Now you listen to me!" she exclaimed. "If this isn't soap opera material, I don't know what is. Just for argument's sake, suppose I have your baby, then what? I turn the child over to you and forget it?"

"We'd share custody."

"How?" she asked, scoffing. "Shuttling back and forth between California and Cape May?"

"Of course not. I'd divide my time. I'd relocate. My crews travel all over the country. It doesn't matter where I live."

In her wildest dreams Katie had never expected to hear such a proposal from Bill. Tendered with love and marriage, she'd gladly nurture his child in her womb, but he hadn't offered either. Worse, she still loved him. The louse!

They'd never dated!

They'd never shared a kiss!

Did he think carrying her up the stairs constituted a courtship!

How dare he! Her mouth tightened. All those wretched years she spent loving a man who still refused to see her as a woman.

She was about to tell him in no uncertain terms what he could do with his plans, when she paused. Mulling over his words, she was surprised at how cynical he sounded about love and marriage. He had been a bit of a Don Juan in high school, but she had assumed he'd outgrow that and one day fall madly in love. Apparently that hadn't happened, and he was determined it never would. Or, she thought, straightening in her chair, he didn't *believe* it would.

She studied him, admitting that the adult Bill was a thousand times more appealing than the teenager had been. Even more, the man had traveled three thousand miles to ask her to have his baby. It might be a crazy idea, but she was flattered he'd chosen her. And maybe if he was willing to have a baby with her, he'd be willing to do a little more. . . .

"For argument's sake," she said in a calm voice, "suppose we explore your proposal. Making babies involves sex. Perhaps once, perhaps many times."

He leapt at the chance to defend his thesis. "It doesn't have to mean anything. Consider the sex part a logical extension of our very good friendship. There's a good chance we won't have to do it often."

She held her breath, her embarrassed gaze sliding away. She refused to allow herself to think of them making love. She's dreamed the steamy scene countless times. Now she put it aside, unwilling to allow it to cloud the issue.

"I think legitimacy is relevant for a child's happiness."

"What are you saying?"

"Simply put," she stated, "should I be insane and consider your business proposition, I insist on marriage . . . for the entire nine months of pregnancy. I'd expect you to be in the delivery room, coaching me through the birth. Afterward, you're off the hook. Hypothetically speaking, that is."

Bill missed the agreeable Katie he remembered, the girl who sought his advice, the girl who needed his approval, his praise. This not-so-agreeable Katie demanded marriage and a baby coach!

"Let me get this straight," he said. "You would agree to have my son if we were married to give the baby legality, then you'd agree to a divorce?"

She shook her head, her mass of red curls bouncing. "Don't jump to conclusions. I said I might. There are considerations."

His eyes hooded suspiciously. "Such as?"

"For openers, a lot depends on the courtship."

"The courtship," he repeated without enthusiasm.

It took great courage to continue, but she plodded on. Given time and opportunity, perhaps she could make him believe in love.

"Courtship. Bill, forget the friendship stuff you've been spouting. I'm not the 'Wham, bam, thank you, ma'am' type. I take it you planned to fit this baby-making business in between trips."

He refused to acknowledge the truth. "Am I to understand you'd consider my request if we were married and I courted you?"

She sat back in her chair. "Put the other way around—courtship first, marriage second—possibly. I refuse to be cheated out of a courtship."

He frowned. "How long?"

She tapped a finger near the corner of her mouth. "I'm not certain. A lot depends on whether I like you."

"You already like me."

"Not the new you."

"I suppose I could reschedule a few things," he said sarcastically.

"There is one other matter," she began.

"I was afraid of that. What is it?"

"Don't flatter yourself that I'd be overwhelmed with gratitude. Pregnancy doesn't do zip to a man's body, except make him feel macho. It does, however, drastically change a woman's body. And the thought of morning sickness isn't especially appealing. The fact is, I hardly know you anymore, and what I've seen and heard leaves a lot to be desired. Frankly, I'm very disappointed in you."

She gazed up at him through thick lashes, then quickly lowered her eyes. Bill was livid. She expected him to storm out of the house. When he didn't, she came to the hard part.

"However, we agree on the state of marriage in today's society. It lacks cohesiveness, commitment. As you say, 'Why be miserable?' I'll admit my age is a factor. My mother was forty-one when she gave birth to me, and it presented certain problems. Like you, I've always loved children—"

"Get to the point."

"Don't rush me. You've had more time to think about this than I have. Now then, there's one item we must clarify before I proceed."

Bill regarded her balefully. In the past Katie had hung onto his words, collecting them like the pearls he'd picked up from the floor. This Katie talked up a storm with no sign of quitting. "And that is?"

"You must complete your end of the bargain first."

He banged his fist on the table. "What? Are you out of your mind? Never! How do I know I can trust you?"

"Will you please stop rattling the glasses. You yourself said we're the best of friends. I may have tricked others when we were growing up, but have I ever tricked you? We put that frog in Charlie's lunch together. Remember? And what about the time when you placed an ad in the newspaper advertising for a new school principal? Who helped you write it?"

"Is there a point to this?"

His eyes burned brightly. She felt heat flow into her from the intensity of gaze. "Indeed. I want to assure you I've never lied to you or tricked you. You have my word. Waiting gives us a chance to renew our friendship. It puts us on a safe footing, if you get my meaning."

"I'm not interested in your feet," he said silkily. "If you get *my* meaning."

By sheer force of will, she managed to add, "In writing. I'll compose a list of rules, then we can discuss them, although I warn you they'll be inflexible."

He frowned. "And that's your idea of negotiations?"

She smiled. "Yes. Considering what you're asking, absolutely."

He sat back, his fingers steepled. For a long while he appeared to be deep in thought, then he abruptly rose and stalked over to her end of the table.

Katie saw the fiery glow in his eyes, heard his

soft laughter. He hovered over her, his fingers gliding up her neck. When they stroked her cheek, then tangled in her hair, she gasped. "What—what are you doing?"

He pulled her out of the chair, hauling her to him. "Sealing our bargain, Katie," he said, his lips a hairbreadth from hers. He kissed her eyes, her cheeks. "I accept your terms, Katie." He nipped the side of her chin. "All of them." His hands slid down her spine. "Your list of rules, the courtship, the marriage, the works." He cupped her buttocks, bringing her hard against him.

"Kiss me, Katie," he demanded. "Kiss me."

His courtship had begun.

# *Three*

Bill's kiss swept Katie into a tumultuous maelstrom that she was helpless to resist. She gave herself up to his masterful caress. He was tall and lithe with strong arms and thighs. His mouth moved against her lips, at first gently, then with increasing urgency. His tongue journeyed inside her mouth, finding, touching, exploring. He lifted her arms around his neck and feasted long and lingeringly on her lips.

Katie moaned softly. Excitement impelled her. She drove her fingers through his thick dark hair, and when she swayed, he drew her closer. He spread his feet wide, nestling her against him, effectively trapping her.

Katie's head whirled. Her heated flesh tingled. Bill was heady wine, more heady than anything she'd ever tasted, but she refused to surrender to temptation. She had loved him from childhood, yearned for him to want her, but not like this. When at last he released her, she looked dazedly into his sapphire eyes, fringed with dark lashes. His gaze held her prisoner as much as his arms. His thumb stroked the edge of her mouth, tracing its contours.

Shaken to the core, furious at being unable to control herself, she blurted out, "That was despicable."

"Didn't you like it?"

She opened her mouth to answer, then clamped her lips together. She couldn't lie, therefore she'd say nothing.

Smiling lazily, he gazed down at her flushed face. In her sparkling eyes, he saw desire at war with confusion. He resisted the impulse to draw her back into his arms and kiss her sweet mouth again. A kiss, he had always maintained, was just a kiss. A vastly enjoyable yet simple pleasure, a temporary igniting of erogenous zones, whose importance too many romantics blew out of proportion. But this kiss he'd shared with Katie went far beyond simple pleasure. It left him wanting to kiss her again and again, and that, he knew, had little to do with conceiving his son. She'd unfairly diverted his thinking.

"I'm following your orders, Katie," he said, sounding calmer than he felt. "Besides, my sweet, a moment ago you weren't acting as though my kiss offended you." He grinned, the corners of his eyes crinkling in boyish mischief. What the hell, he thought. What crime was there in having a little pleasure too?

Expanding on this he said, "Those were your fingers I felt in my hair, your breasts pressed to my chest, your tongue dueling with mine. I'd say you enjoyed yourself too."

"Spoken like a true gentleman!" she exclaimed, jerking out of his hold. To her horror, Bill lifted her up and planted another quick kiss on her mouth. Grinning, he let her go.

She smoothed her dress. "Let's eat. I'm hungry."

"Whatever you say, Katie." His lips quirked in a ready laugh.

"Hah!"

"Katie."

"What?" she asked, feeling her face heat.

His eyes darkened. He drew his thumb across her bottom lip. He'd never noticed before how luscious it was, even a little pouty. "I think this courtship might just turn out to be fun."

Or a disaster! Katie thought.

They ate a buffet dinner at the Huntington House, one of the oldest operating hotels in Cape May. Bill devoured his hearty meal, sampling freely from the appetizers, salads, and entrees, before ending his dinner with two desserts and coffee.

Katie picked at her food.

"You know," he said, after demolishing his second dessert, "the wide hanging staircase in this hotel is the oldest of its type in the country. You're not going to find a post or a visible support. Be sure to notice the chestnut wood when we leave. It's magnificent."

Katie's annoyance was reaching an overflow level. During the ride over, Bill had acted nonchalant, as if kissing a woman until her knees turned to water was an everyday occurrence, from which he recovered nicely and quickly.

"Bill, shouldn't we first discuss this?"

"Don't worry." His smile blazed. "I wouldn't

think of using chestnut wood in your house. We'll follow the original plans. We're historical ,detectives. We snoop into the past, uncovering and restoring treasures. If you have a copy of the blueprints, let me have them later. If not, the Historical Society may have a duplicate on file. Frankly, I prefer the Queen Anne Victorian, like yours, to the Gothic-style Victorian."

Katie's gaze veered to the knife near her plate. With very little urging she'd cheerfully slit his throat.

"I tell you," he added enthusiastically, "it's great to be home." He patted her hand. "And speaking specifically of your home, I'll hire the best artisans money can buy. They'll replace the brackets, scrolls, frets, bargeboards, and the gables. Once the house is painted and the latticework around the base of the porch is replaced, you won't recognize the place. I'll have the entire structure checked for termites, unless you've had a recent check. Have you, Katie?"

She didn't trust herself to speak. She just listened, her small hands clenching into fists.

"Katie, you're not eating," he noted. "Eat. You want to keep up your strength. Our son needs a healthy mother. I don't like women without flesh on their bones. That's okay for models or actresses, but not mothers."

She was determined not to scream, but it was getting harder by the second. Bill proceeded, undaunted by the strangled sound coming from her throat. "In the old days," he said, "to accent their skill, the various craftsmen painted each architectural detail a different color. They'll have a field day with your house. When everything's done I'll hire a landscape architect. We'll spruce up the outside. Have you noticed the rhododendron in your yard are dying? We'll plant new ones. Wait until you see how the outside perks up with new bushes and flowers."

"Oh, for goodness' sake, stop!" she snapped. "Are you really so obtuse?"

He apologized immediately. "Forgive me. I didn't mean to hurt your feelings. You couldn't help letting your house sink into such a state of disrepair, not with all your financial troubles. I thought you'd be pleased to know I intend to take care of everything."

She drew in a deep breath. "Bill, are we here to discuss remodelling?"

He contemplated her serious visage, noting also her clasped hands and whitened knuckles. He kept his tone purposely light.

"You'd prefer we discuss another topic. Fine. Suppose we talk about our son."

Katie kicked him under the table. "Be quiet!" She waited for the busboy to clear the table, then leaned forward. "Why did you kiss me like that?"

His eyes flashed fiercely, then cooled. Taking her hand in his, he unfurled her fingers one by one. Then he slowly lifted her hand and dropped a heated kiss into the center of her palm. "Was kissing me so awful, Katie?"

"No," she admitted, withdrawing her tingling hand from his. She fought the myriad sensations Bill evoked in her. Just the sight of him took her breath away. Part of her irritation stemmed from his failing to comment on her appearance. She knew she looked good in her black dress. It dramatically set off her red hair and her figure. She had taken special pains with her makeup. Yet even when he'd helped her on with her wool coat, then placed his hand at the small of her back as they walked down the path to his car, he hadn't commented on her appearance.

"So why should we quibble?" he asked. "I admit I enjoyed kissing you. You don't deny you enjoyed kissing me. What's the big deal?"

She glanced around the crowded restaurant. Families occupied many of the tables. Bill followed her gaze. He smiled. She didn't.

"You're taking too much for granted, Bill. We're still at the hypothetical stage."

He hunched forward, bringing his face close to hers. "Uh, uh. The kiss said otherwise. We're at the courtship stage."

"Sit back," she ordered. "People are beginning to stare. You thought wrong, Bill. I'm at the dating stage."

He smiled faintly at that. Whether Katie realized it or not, she was on her way to making a commitment. "What's the difference? Why waste time?"

Katie hesitated. After his devastating kiss, she knew herself well enough to realize her plan to have him fall in love with her wouldn't stand a chance if she didn't keep both of them in check. She searched for an excuse, and at last blurted out, "Liberties. It strikes me that you're a man who likes his way."

"I admit I'm a man on a mission. I want a son. I want to be a father. I have the instinct for it. I'm planning on being a great father. I don't mind changing diapers. While we're discussing impressions, it strikes me that you've become damned unreasonable, or at the very least, obstinate."

Her brows knitted together in displeasure. She was angry with herself for not having the sense to tell him to take a flying leap. "You're right," she agreed, stalling. "I am obstinate. And I'm putting *no kissing* at the top of the list."

His head jerked up. "For how long?"

She saw the feral gleam in his eyes and moved quickly to squelch it. "Until I'm ready." She swallowed hard, then forced herself to speak persuasively. "Have I your word?"

He shifted his position. "In a word, no." He was obviously getting irritated. "Katie, you cannot expect me to agree to that silly order without first knowing if it will be worth my effort."

She stared at his hands. They were strong and large, with long, tapered fingers. The thought of them caressing her body made her shiver. "Why did you choose me? I'm sure there are women where you live. Women who would gladly trade their bodies for security."

He grabbed her hands. She tried to extricate them, but he tightened his grip, as if to make sure she stayed put. "Katie, get this straight. I'm not buying you. I never intended for you to think such a deplorable thing. You have free choice. Katie, I like you. I've always liked you."

Angered, she pulled free of his grasp. "How else should I interpret your proposition? This isn't about love. It's about bartering."

He shook his head. "Think of it as two old friends, very good, dear friends, who will be giving each other a gift. A gift of life for a child who will be loved. Despite what you think of my proposal, I never considered another woman. Don't forget, we go back a long way. I know you'll make a great mother. We're two single people. Why complicate matters with grand statements of love?"

"What have you got against love?" she asked.

"Nothing," he said expansively. "For some people it's the greatest thing going. For me it hasn't happened. That's not to say there haven't been women in my life, or times I thought maybe it was the real thing, but it never turned out to be love."

"Why not?"

"Why not what?"

"Why haven't you been able to have a lasting relationship?"

That caught Bill up short. He'd always told himself, whenever he bothered to look over his track record with women, that he'd never fallen in love because the women were never right. Yet the way Katie phrased the question, it sounded as though there might be something wrong with him, not the women. Discomfited, he cleared his throat.

"Being a realist," he said, "I decided to go after what I want. A 'lasting relationship' is not a prerequisite for being a father, and the only lack I feel in my life right now is a son. Not love. Can you honestly say love lasts longer than friendship, because if you can, you're lying."

Katie listened attentively to what she determined was eloquent drivel, offered by a man whose husky voice and seductive eyes were turning her insides to jelly. "I prefer seeing the world as half-full, not half-empty."

"Good. Women are supposed to be dreamers. I'll remain the realist."

"Why do you want my decision now?"

"According to my calculations, the youngest I

could be when I meet our son is thirty-three. Add seven years until he's old enough to play football, that makes me forty. Suppose we decide to have another baby when our son is three or four. You surely wouldn't want him to be an only child?" The question was intended to be rhetorical, which was just as well since Katie was beyond speech. "I remember," Bill went on, "when we confided to each other that we wished we had a sister or a brother. Okay, you become pregnant again when I'm thirty-six or thirty-seven. Adding nine months for the pregnancy, I could be as old as forty-five before our second son plays football."

Appalled, she let her mouth drop open.

"Forty-five-year-old knees are out of condition. My knees are the main reason I need to get started right away." He paused, then added, "Shall I calculate your age, or would you prefer to subtract by two?"

Katie half rose from her seat and wagged her finger at him. "No *daughter* of mine will have her precious body hurt playing football. Since when have you become interested in football? You never played it."

As she rattled on, her voice rose, to the delight of the people listening at a nearby table. "Our daughter will excel in swimming. Swimming is a nice, safe sport. It's good enough for us, it's good enough for her. Making a baby to satisfy your nutty time-line is out! Totally, completely out! And where do you come off asking for two?"

Bill's shoulders shook with mirth. He tried and failed to check his laugh. Mortified, Katie realized what she had said. She felt her cheeks flame as she eased back into her chair.

"I was merely pointing out the necessity to remember my age. My clock's ticking," he added, insinuating hers was too. He ducked when she appeared ready to throw her spoon. "Calm yourself. You want our son to swim, he'll swim. I've never seen you like this, Katie. You used to be amenable."

"You mean manageable," she retorted. "I must have been a fool."

He raised his hands in a gesture of conciliation. "All right. I won't rush you. I promise. We'll resume kissing in three days if waiting makes you feel better. I'll stop talking about babies. I just hope you realize how agreeable I am. You see, it's over. End of conversation. I'll tell you what. We'll change the subject. We'll talk about something safe." He snapped his fingers. "I know. Let's talk about Phyllis. You said she works for you. How is she these days?"

Groaning, Katie flopped back in her chair. Her hands hung limply by her sides. "Pregnant," she muttered. "These days Phyllis is seven months pregnant with her second child."

His face split with an instant grin. "Let's hope it's catching."

"Oh, shut up," she mumbled, but her eyes softened. In the face of Bill's clouded judgement, she saw her task clearly. He needed her to set him on the path to lasting happiness!

In the years that Katie had lived alone, she had kept busy socially, but that had lessened as the demands of her fledgling business increased. Phyllis counseled her to date more, saying she needed the balance. She did. Yet at odd times, Katie caught herself wondering about Bill, how she'd react if she ever saw him again. If this was any indication of her reaction to him, she was in serious trouble. As they were putting on their coats to leave the restaurant, she reminded herself yet again of Phyllis's warning about Bill. She'd be wise to heed it.

Bill took her elbow and guided her outside. "Would you like to walk a while?"

She nodded. She needed a dose of fresh air to clear her head.

They strolled along the promenade by the ocean, reminiscing about the days when they would pile into his old car and drive to Wildwood Crest. They would wander the noisy boardwalk, stopping at the carnival booths to test their skill.

"I won a Kewpie doll for you, Katie."

She smiled, feeling the tension ebb out of her. "I haven't thought about that doll in years. I must still have it packed away in the attic."

He circled his arm around her shoulders. "You tried to win a radio for me."

"I would have, too," she protested, "if the barker had played honestly. I'm convinced those machines are programmed to cheat."

The wind picked up, whipping her coat around her legs. Bill tucked her cold hand into his pocket and held the other.

"Oh, look!" she cried softly. A tiny brown-and-white kitten was hurrying over to them, mewing. She bent to pet its soft fur. "The poor little thing," she said, picking the kitten up.

"Hello, little one," she cooed. "Have you lost your mother?" The kitten purred its response.

The little animal rubbed its head against Katie's palm, delighting her and Bill. Its purr settled into a low, continuous rumble.

"You always were a softie for strays," Bill said.

She stroked the kitten's ears. "It's awfully cold. How would you like to come home with me for a few days?" The kitten blinked. "I take it that means yes." Bundling her furry charge inside her coat, she gazed up at Bill.

He gave up his plan to buy her a dog. Seeing the glow in her eyes, he couldn't resist caressing her cheek.

"If I purr and rub against you," he murmured, "will you take me home for a few days too?"

She playfully bumped his hip. "You never give up, do you? I'll take you as far as the front door."

"I might have guessed," he groused good-naturedly, and Katie knew their walk had lessened the strain of the evening's conversation. They could still joke and enjoy each other's company.

They hurried to his car. Bill threw it in gear and flipped on the heater. The kitten purred contentedly on Katie's lap the whole way home. Inside the house, Katie made a bed for the animal out of a box and an old pillow, setting it in the kitchen. She tore up newspaper and layered it in another box, in lieu of cat litter. As she introduced the kitten to its temporary home, Bill peered at the cupboards, inside and out, then down at the floor.

"This is a great room," he said, gazing around it. "It has wonderful possibilities."

Katie agreed. For relaxation on sunny weekend mornings she baked bread and batches of oatmeal-raisin cookies. "There's something comforting about kitchens," she said, leaning against the counter. A line of potted herbs stood on the deep-silled window beside her.

"It's the heart of the house. That and the bedroom." He smiled. "Your mother used to bake cookies for me. I bet you didn't remember that, did you?"

"I bet I did. Mom's oatmeal-and-raisin cookies were my favorite too. I was the one who asked her to bake extra for you so that you'd stop stealing mine." She opened a ceramic cookie jar. Bill's eyes lit up with pleasure. "Try mine," she said.

"They were good days, Katie," he said, munching on a cookie. "I guess I lost track of them. This is delicious." He helped himself to a second cookie. "What color would you like the new cupboards and the counters?"

"I hadn't thought about it," she said, forgetting the reason behind his question. She poured milk into a bowl for the kitten. "Yellow," she said, setting the bowl on the floor. "A buttery yellow for the cupboards and white tile countertops."

"Done." Bill swiped a third cookie. "The floors are going to be ripped up too. You might as well think in terms of the whole kitchen. The stove and refrigerator go."

Katie let her mind drift. Having carte blanche to fix up her home was like winning the lottery. You never think it could happen to you. Idly, she traced a finger around a dill plant. "It would be nice to see the house the way it used to be," she said. "With fresh paint and the floors sanded and varnished, the banister and newels tightened, the house will look spectacular."

"Don't forget about the lighting fixtures," Bill

said. "They'll need rewiring. We can modernize the bathrooms and still retain the Victorian decor."

"Oh, my gosh!" she exclaimed, catching herself from adding that the windows could use new curtains. "Listen to me prattle." She tamped down her excitement. "I'm getting ahead of myself."

Deeming it wise not to push it, Bill said nothing and turned his attention to the kitten. Both he and Katie laughed as the little animal polished the bowl clean. Within minutes, the exhausted kitten curled up on his pillow and fell asleep.

Bill said good night with a polite handshake, throwing Katie into an uncharacteristically gloomy mood. Feeling deprived, she wished he had kissed her so that she could have chastised him for rushing things. She trudged dispiritedly through her bedroom and flung open the door to the belvedere. As she stepped into the bracing air, she was just in time to glimpse the taillights of Bill's car, watching until he rounded a corner.

Shivering, she scooted back into her bedroom, kicked off her shoes, and slumped down on the bed. It had been an incredible night. Even now she could hardly believe it. What had she let herself in for? Thinking back over the evening, she realized she had led him to believe she had accepted his deal. After all, she hadn't refused. All she had done was to set a few stumbling blocks in his path. She'd set limits that he'd agreed to abide by, yet she should write them down, with a copy for each.

Her head filled with questions, she undressed and changed into a flannel nightgown, then headed into the bathroom to wash. Coming out, she stopped to get her yearbook from the shelf.

Flipping through it, she stared at the pictures of Bill. Bill snapped with the swim team. Bill hunched over a desk. Bill grinning. There was even one of Bill with her.

Crawling into bed, Katie lay alone between the sheets with the light of the moon streaming through the lace curtains. She cursed herself for wanting him, now more than ever. During the night she dreamed of Bill, calculating his age as they wheeled her into the delivery room to give birth to their fifth daughter!

The following morning she awoke to the combined sounds of her alarm clock's shrill buzzer, the television's automatic timer bringing her the six-o'clock news, and the mewing kitten. Before leaving for work, she fed him and made a note to stop at the store to buy cat food and kitty litter. Only when she was behind the wheel of her car did she admit to herself how much she looked forward to seeing Bill again.

"How was your date last night?" Phyllis asked the moment she entered Katie's office. She moved letters aside to make room on the desk for two coffee containers and two bagels. "I was dying to call you last night, but Fred told me to mind my own business." She laughed. "The heck with him. Tell me everything, Katie. Don't leave anything out. Is Bill still good-looking? Did he get fat and ugly?"

Katie brought the steaming cup of liquid to her lips. She felt languid, disconnected. "Bill's gorgeous. He's virile and lean. He's unmarried. He hasn't lost his eye-catching good looks. I think I'm having a baby."

Phyllis's hand shot out to feel Katie's forehead. "Do you know a rabbit I don't? I could swear I heard you say you're having a baby."

Katie dabbed her lips with a napkin. "Bill's worried about his knees, Phil."

Phyllis snatched Katie's bagel. "Maybe you ought to go home and lie down. You're not making sense. Keep away from the phone and don't answer the doorbell. Above all, refuse to see Bill. Then you'll recover."

"No," she assured Phyllis. "I'm fine. It's Bill. He's anxious to have a son."

Phyllis looked confused. "Good for him, I think. But what does that have to do with his knees?"

"He's worried they'll give out by the time he's forty-five."

"Katie!" Phyllis said sharply. "Stop teasing me and talk! No sane man worries about forty-five-year-old knees at the age of thirty-two. That is Bill's age, isn't it?"

Katie picked up the bagel and munched it thoughtfully. "Believe me, Phil, as nutty as it sounds, I'm telling the truth. Bill's knees have a direct relationship with his desire to father a son at this time."

"That's impossible," Phyllis stated. "Heck, it's not even romantic."

Katie shrugged. "You think that's not romantic? Listen to this." She launched into a recital of Bill's baby time-line theory. She had to backtrack twice, getting mixed up between the ages and the dates. Phyllis dissolved into a fit of laughter. Each time she attempted speaking she fell into gales of merriment. Katie handed her a tissue to wipe her eyes.

"It's not funny," she said, failing utterly to keep the mirth out of her own voice.

"That's what you think. I can't believe his nerve. Cut the nonsense, tell me what you really said."

"I told him I'd consider it."

Phyllis sucked in her breath. "Will wonders never cease! Katie, how could you?"

"You weren't there. Bill's very persuasive. Anyway, I've thought of a plan to ensure that he keeps his distance."

"Take it from me, honey." Phyllis rolled her hands protectively around her stomach. "If you two expect to make a baby, distance doesn't work. I can't believe this." She started chuckling again.

"I'm glad I'm entertaining you," Katie said stiffly.

"You are. Nothing exciting happens to me. Maybe you two were cut out for each other. Are you still in love with him?"

"Who knows? I loved him years ago. He certainly turns me on."

"When does he want this baby?"

"Son," Katie corrected her. "According to his time-line, as soon as possible."

"Amazing," Phyllis exclaimed. "All these years he's out of your life. Suddenly he realizes he's in love with you, flies here to state his love, asks you to marry him, and can't wait to start a family."

Katie cleared her throat. The echo of the previous night's conversation rang in her ears. Although she was a grown woman, capable of making her own decisions, she wanted Phyllis's understanding and, she hoped, her approval.

"Bill isn't in love with me. He's not even in lust with me. He's in *like* with me. It was my idea to marry, not his. You might say I backed him into a corner. He had to agree or I wouldn't."

Phyllis flared indignantly.

Katie tossed the bagel aside. She'd lost her appetite. "Don't say it, Phil. I've already given myself all the scoldings I can tolerate. You have no idea how glad I am my folks aren't in town."

Phyllis frowned. "I suppose women marry for worse reasons. As you say, he likes you. Heaven knows, like often lasts longer than love."

"You're beginning to sound like him."

Phyllis got up to stretch. "Liking your husband is important in a marriage. Fred and I like each other as well as love each other. You'll certainly have a load off your mind knowing he'll make you financially secure. Bill's successful, but then he was always good at whatever he attempted. When is the ceremony taking place?"

Katie brushed crumbs from the desk and tidied her papers. "It's not. At least not until I say so. In the meantime, he's going to read a list of rules I'm writing. He'll sign them."

"A list of rules?" Phyllis asked, stupefied. "He agreed to sign a list of rules he hasn't read?"

"Yes, in principle. We've talked about it in general. For starters, I want a courtship. The more I think about the days when we were growing up, the more I realize I shouldn't have faulted Bill for not seeing me as a girlfriend. We were just two friends who grew up in the same neighborhood and swam on the same team and joined the same club."

"And now?" Phyllis asked. "You're not kids any-more. Look, Katie, I know how much you've always wanted a family. It's one of the reasons you're such a willing listener when I tell you about Charlie's latest antics. Your face lights up when you play with him. Each time you dated a man for more than a month I hoped he was the one. For some women there's only one man. For you it may be Bill. I'll even grant you he'll probably make a wonderful father. But this . . . ?"

Katie drew in a deep breath for reassurance and let it out slowly. "Time will tell, won't it. This may be the greatest cure going. How many women have a second chance at love? Besides, it's entirely possible I'll find out I've never really loved Bill, that all these years I mistook infatuation for love. Or, it's possible Bill will fall in love with me. That alone is a worthwhile reason to play this out, isn't it?"

Phyllis's eyes crinkled with laughter. "Fred and I had such an unconventional courtship. All we did was meet, fall in love, and get married."

"In our case, half is true," Katie said. "I fell in love. Bill's worried about his knees."

"Look on the bright side," Phyllis countered. "Bill wants *you*. My goodness! The man's flown across the country to get you. Hasn't it occurred to you that after all these years he's come home to you like a homing pigeon?"

Katie unwrapped a piece of chocolate and popped it into her mouth, smiling impishly. "That's what I'm counting on. Bill believes friend-ship is the basis of lasting relationships. 'Why muck up the waters with marriage?' according to him."

"But he's willing to marry you."

"It's the modern version of a shotgun marriage. It isn't the same as the balcony scene from *Romeo and Juliet*. Every woman wants to be courted for herself, not her reproduction machinery."

"You're being too hard on yourself, Katie."

She shook her head. "Bill knows I love kids. We used to talk about the future, what each of us hoped would happen. Workwise, he's accomplished his goal. He specializes in restoring old houses. Becoming a father is another goal, one he can't accomplish alone. So he thought of me— good old Katie. As teenagers we talked about being only children, how we wished we had come from large families. Bill remembered."

"Then don't you think it's strange he only wants one child?"

Katie chuckled. "Actually, I'm certain he'd like two—without the benefit of traditional hearth and home. I absolutely refused. Unless I can teach him to believe and trust in love, I'm going to be one of the few brides entering a marriage with a prearranged divorce. It's either complicated or simple. I haven't figured out which."

"It's crazy, but it's not hopeless, Katie. The Bill I remember had a lot going for him besides looks."

Katie pondered her friend's remark. "This Bill is all man. He's also highly competitive."

"You're highly competitive too. Is this contract being drawn up by a lawyer?"

"Absolutely not," Katie replied. "You're sworn to secrecy. I don't want this to get around. Other than you, and he's aware I intended to tell you, I prefer to keep our unconventional arrangement private."

Phyllis patted her arm. "Be careful not to give away too much too fast."

Katie felt her face heat. Considering Bill's scorching kiss and her active response, she needed to be vigilant. "Trust me, Phil, I'm not giving away anything. Bill agreed to stick to the rules."

"And you believed him?"

Katie uncrossed her legs and crossed her fingers.

# *Four*

A bouquet of yellow daisies and yellow roses arrived for Katie at noon. "What in the world!" Phyllis and Katie cried in unison. Katie dove for the card.

" 'Three days no kissing unfair,' " she read aloud. " 'Not sure I can accept conditions.' "

She hugged the card to her bosom as though it were a book of love sonnets. "They're from Bill."

"What does he mean by three days?" Phyllis asked.

"Oh, nothing," Katie replied offhandedly. She scouted in her office for a vase. When she returned she waited on a customer. Phyllis, never one to leave unanswered questions dangling, repeated hers.

"What's the three days refer to?"

"I stipulated that he has to wait three days before he can kiss me again. I'm trying to build Bill's character. He's used to having his wishes instantly fulfilled, I think."

Phyllis shook her head in amazement. "You two are original. I'll say that for you."

A music box arrived at one o'clock. It played *Brahms' Lullaby*. Katie rewound it four times.

"I take it the lullaby is supposed to get you in the mood," Phyllis said. "It's killing mine." She locked it away in a closet.

A large box, filled to the brim with copies of Dr. Seuss books, arrived at two o'clock. "Now this is more like it," Phyllis said approvingly. "My son will love these. I'll return them when yours is old enough to read."

Shortly before closing, Bill himself strolled in. He carried about him a kind of raw energy, an electricity, an aura of commanding strength. Katie's heart skipped as it always did when she saw him. He wore jeans and a sweatshirt, and his hands rested comfortably in the pockets of an old navy peacoat. He favored both women with a high-potency grin.

To her surprise, he formally shook her hand, then wrapped his arms about Phyllis and gave her a big bear hug. His gaze traveled down to her stomach. "Congratulations on the baby. I'd kiss Katie but I'm not allowed. I'm in the doghouse for three days."

"I heard," Phyllis said dryly.

He rocked back on his heels. "Trust me, I have no intention of staying there."

Katie threw up her hands. He was clearly teasing her, but then she felt his fingers lift her ponytail and linger on the nape of her neck. She hoped he didn't realize how his innocent touch made her tremble, however slightly. She took his jacket to hang it up. "Thank you for the presents," she said.

"You're welcome. Oh, by the way, I stopped at a Chinese restaurant and picked up a few things for dinner."

He made a thorough tour of Sweet Mischief. With Katie's permission, he also helped himself to several pieces of candy.

"How much longer are you going to work, Phyllis?" he asked. "Shouldn't you be home taking it easy?"

"Contrary to popular opinion, pregnancy is a condition, not an illness. I plan on working up to the last minute."

"Who's taking your place?"

"Sally Knudsen," Katie said. "Eric Knudsen's wife. You remember Eric, don't you?"

Bill nodded. "That's great. Sally's a nice person. Listen, I'm starved and the food's getting cold. How much longer will you be?"

"Give me time to tally the drawer first," Katie said. She was heading for the register when she heard the door open and Bill's enthusiastic greeting.

"Well, hello. Don't you look beautiful."

Katie swung around to see Bill's one-time girl-friend, Janice Mortman Ramirez, sidle up to him and wrap one sinuous arm about his neck. Janice exuded sexual heat with as much fire as a stoked furnace. A predator, she had succeeded in landing two husbands in ten years. She'd divorced the first when his money ran out. Her second husband had died, leaving her richly widowed and childless. The only thing that had changed about Janice since they were kids, Katie thought miserably, was that Janice was even more of a femme fatale now. She went after men with single-minded purpose. Tall, with a model's elegant carriage, she wore an amber cashmere sheath and over it a rust-colored cashmere cape. In her denim skirt and blue cotton sweater, Katie felt dowdy compared to Janice. The brown-eyed, ebony-haired beauty had eyes only for Bill. Her body movements said *I want this man and what I want I get.* She kissed him full on the mouth.

"Darling," she said, still clinging to him, "I couldn't believe my eyes. Welcome home. Isn't it marvelous, Katie? Bill's come back to us. Will you be staying long?"

"A while," he said, extricating himself from her.

Her hot, dark eyes, hooded with shadow and liner, seemed to possess him. "Wonderful, darling. Give me your number. We'll get together soon and renew old times. Katie, give me a piece of paper." She tucked her address and number into his pocket.

Katie was instantly offended. Janice was making no effort to hide her delight in seeing Bill. Ignoring Katie, she rested a proprietary hand on his shoulder.

"I'll leave you two," Katie said, feeling helplessly out of her league. Bill had looked at Janice as if she were one of the delectable pieces of chocolate in the display case. Apparently he still viewed Janice as drop-dead beautiful, while her major asset was that of a brood mare! "Go on with your reunion," she mumbled. "I've got orders to process."

Within minutes Phyllis joined her in the office. She closed the door behind her. "Not smart, Katie."

"Please, don't you start on me."

"Somebody should. You lost your cool. It wasn't Bill's fault that Janice came on to him like gangbusters."

"Earlier today you thought I was nuts," Katie said, defending herself. "Now all of a sudden, you're taking Bill's side!"

"I'm still on your side, silly. In your heart you want this man, yet at the first sign of competition, you fold. Shame on you. The moment Janice learns Bill is single, she'll go after him like a piranha."

Katie aimed a sideways glance at Phyllis. "As if a man being married would stop her! As far as I'm concerned they can have each other. I ought to count my blessings this happened now, before I really made a fool of myself."

She wished she could sneak out the back door and not have to endure the sight of Janice climbing all over an all-too-willing Bill. She glared angrily at the unopened mail on her desk, then looked up when she heard the door open. Bill stood there, motioning to Phyllis to leave them alone.

"You're mad," he stated when Phyllis was gone.

Fighting back tears, she bravely lifted her chin. "Dogs get mad; people get angry."

"You're angry."

"No, I'm not," she lied. Sensations she didn't want to feel fluttered inside her. "Why should I be?"

He settled his large frame against the wall. "Beats me."

Katie slammed shut her desk drawer and yanked open a file drawer. "I run a place of business. How would it have looked if a customer had come in and seen you kissing Janice?"

He folded his arms across his chest. "I didn't kiss her. She kissed me."

"You always were sweet on her," she blurted out, and immediately wished she had kept quiet.

"She took me by surprise. What was I supposed to do? Sock her in the jaw?"

Katie dug her fists into her waist. "Very funny!"

He moved swiftly across the room, picked her up, and perched her on top of the desk. Bracketing her body with his arms, he brought his face within an inch of hers, irking her further when she sniffed his appealing cologne.

"You're jealous," he said. "Ordinarily I'd appreciate it, but not tonight. Use your head. Would I kiss another woman in front of you?"

"As long as it's not in front of me it's all right, is that it?"

"Stop picking apart my words, dammit! I sent those gifts to you, not Janice."

"Because you didn't know she was available. You've got her number. Go after her. Take your gifts with you."

He bent his head, his lips nearly touching hers. His eyes glinted dangerously. "Katie, I've had a long and busy day making plans for us, plans that I had hoped to discuss with you. We've got a lot to do. So if you don't mind, count the drawer and let's get out of here. Furthermore, I'm hungry. I imagine the kitten is too."

"Go to hell!" Katie said, deliberately baiting him.

"Not without the mother of my son," he said meaningfully. He peered into her rebellious face.

"We have a deal. I won't allow your redheaded temper to kill it. Last night, after I returned to my hotel, I made the necessary phone calls to bring in a crew of talented people. Sy Baxter, my foreman, is arriving tomorrow. So let go of your snit, Katie, my girl. You may be getting a boarder."

Her ears perked up at that. "What do you mean?" she asked, momentarily diverted. "Who?"

"Sy Baxter hates being away from home. He's a family man. It's one of the things I wanted to discuss with you. You've got bedrooms going to waste. I prevailed upon him to take this job. If he's at the house, he'll be less lonely. There's another plus. He'll be right there at all times, overseeing everything."

She stared at him in amazement. Bill proceeded full steam ahead while she preferred taking things slowly, letting matters progress gradually.

"I won't have a strange man in my house. I live alone. What would people think?"

He smiled, and she could swear the devil glinted in his eyes. "You won't be alone. I'll be there too."

"What!" She forgot all about Janice. "Bill, you can't!"

"Of course I can. I consider it my duty to protect you. How will it look if the neighbors see a strange man living with you?"

"That's what I said."

"Exactly. You know this town. Everyone gossips. You don't run a bed-and-breakfast. With your being a merchant here, I have to protect your honor."

"By living with me?" she asked, stunned. "As you said, neighbors talk. What do you intend to tell them about you, if it isn't too much to ask?"

He tugged her ponytail. "The truth, of course. We'll tell them we're getting married, that we're fixing up the house. No one need know the rest of our arrangement. I'm a hometown boy. They'll think it's wonderful. We'll have a party to celebrate the house after it's fixed up. We'll invite the old gang and anyone else you want."

Katie shook her head in disbelief. Bill's whirlwind actions left her flabbergasted. In twenty-four hours he'd commandeered her house by finagling an invitation for his foreman, and drummed up an excuse for himself, too, in the guise of protecting her sterling reputation.

Katie thought fast. For every step he took, she'd take two. She raised her eyes to Bill's. A guileless smile tugged at the corners of his mouth. He really thought he'd pulled a fast one. She quickly realized that Janice was the least of her problems!

Her instincts advised her to quit while she was ahead, to forget her love for Bill and her hopes he'd fall in love with her. Unfortunately, her heart warred with her instincts, and her heart won.

She renewed her determination to fight fire with fire—his sneaky plan with her sneakier one. The sudden urge to laugh was so overwhelming, she clapped her hand over her mouth and pretended to sneeze. She was gratified Bill couldn't read her mind.

"I suppose I did get a bit carried away before," she said, hopping off the desk. "I'll be pleased to have your foreman at the house. Naturally I understand why you want to be there too."

"Now you're my agreeable Katie. I forgive you for flying off the handle," he said charitably. Encouraged by her returning good humor, Bill did what he'd been wanting to do ever since he'd walked into the store. Gently grasping her chin between his forefinger and his thumb, he tipped her face up to his as he lowered his head. She drew a shuddering breath. "Don't count it toward the three-day moratorium. This is a make-up kiss."

"How generous," she murmured, sliding her hands up his chest, surrendering to the stormy passion in her heart. She kissed him with all her love, hoping it wouldn't betray her.

When at last Bill lifted his mouth from hers, his mind was cloudy with confusion. His feelings for Katie were changing, he realized, but he had no idea what they were changing into.

Phyllis poked her head in, checked to see the furniture was still in place, then came all the way in and sat down. "Whew, I'm tired," she said, wiggling her feet. "I'm ready to leave, Katie. Is everything okay with you two?"

Katie permitted herself the luxury of snuggling up to Bill. "Bill's foreman is staying at my place. Bill's eager to start on the house right away. And guess what?"

"What?" Phyllis asked dubiously.

Katie allowed her adoring gaze to linger on Bill. "Bill's moving in to protect my reputation."

Phyllis snorted. "Figures."


The supermarket Katie stopped in on the way home was filled with early evening shoppers. She informed a hungry, disgruntled Bill that she'd fed the kitten, assured him that the Chinese food would keep, then tripped along ahead of him.

"I want to do my part," she said, ignoring the

rumbling growl from his stomach. "You acted so swiftly, so decisively, making good on your promise to restore my home, the least I can do is show my good faith too." She smothered a laugh.

Acting like a bride, Katie dragged Bill up and down food aisles, pausing to check on the merits of each purchase and awaiting his approval.

"You know your foreman. Do you think he'll like this?"

"How should I know?" Bill muttered. He had come up with his brainstorm at the last minute. With Katie threatening him with a list of rules and regulations, he'd had to change his strategy. "No one's asking you to feed him. Sy'll eat in a restaurant. Don't you want to know what I like?"

"I already know what you like," she replied coyly.

Next she insisted on stopping at the department store. When Bill complained of hunger, she solicitously handed him a packet of crushed saltines.

"I always keep one or two packets in my purse," she said. Inside the store, she took her time shopping, reminding him that he should be grateful she compared prices. "You should be glad that I won't waste your money."

She cheerfully piled Bill's arms with bed linens, towels, soaps, and tissues. Next she headed for the bedding department.

She ordered two twin mattresses and box springs, explaining to Bill that the ones in the spare rooms were lumpy. She chose pillows and spreads to be delivered the following day. But she almost fainted when Bill suddenly pulled her down on a king-size bed and threw his arms around her, in full view of the salesman.

"We might as well try it out as long as we're here," he said. Her eyes widened, and he laughed. Flustered, Katie scrambled off the bed.

He caught up to her in two long strides. "We're not making our son standing up or in a twin bed. Your delaying tactics won't do a bit of good. This shopping spree constitutes our first date. And Katie, I like the fact that you keep saltines in your purse. Buy more. Keep a box in the store."

"Why"

He responded in a flash. "I'm told it lessens the effects of morning sickness."

If she were keeping score, Katie thought gloomily, it would read Bill 3, Katie 0.

When they finally reached her house, Bill unloaded the car, then helped Katie put the groceries away. She heated the Chinese food, boiled water for tea, and set the table, placing Bill's flowers in the center. Excited to have some company, the kitten acted as if he owned the house, darting in corners, finding pieces of fallen plaster to play with. He scampered between Bill's legs, giving him a hard time as Bill lugged the mattresses upstairs to the rooms he and Sy would occupy.

"We're going to have to give this guy a name," Bill said when he joined her. "It looks as if he's taken up residence."

The kitten batted a ball of twine and showed off.

"Samson's a good name," she said.

"Samson it is. As long as it's for the kitten and not our son. I remember what Delilah did to Samson."

Katie took the statement without comment,

handing Bill an envelope. "I drew this up early this morning. It's your copy of the list of rules for our business arrangement. Why don't you read it over?" She ladled wonton soup into their bowls.

Bill set the paper aside. "I'm sure the list covers the basics. Courtship. Marriage. Baby. Divorce." He sipped his soup, added a dash of mustard. "I trust you, Katie. You'd never cheat me. We both know this is a good deal. Pass the noodles, please."

She asked for the hot mustard.

He asked for the soy sauce.

He read his fortune cookie.

She read hers.

They shared the meal like any two civilized people who didn't know what they were eating.

Her brain clicked at one hundred miles per hour. She did not envision herself divorced.

His clicked just as fast. He did not envision himself married, at least not permanently.

Bill leaned back in his chair and studied her. Ever since he's first kissed her, he had been bothered by a vague sense of something amiss. His goals were starting to blur. If he were interested only in having a son, why was Katie taking up so much of his thoughts? And why, when you got right down to it, had he finagled his way into her house?

"Katie," he said as an old twinge of guilt assailed him, "another reason it's wise for me to stay here is because it's easier to run my business from a house than a small hotel room."

"Of course," she murmured. "I realize you need to spread out. I do hope you'll be comfortable on the new mattress. Perhaps we should have gotten a larger size. You are a big man. I know I like to move around in bed."

"The twin is fine," he said, his voice a bit hoarse. "You're really very agreeable. I appreciate your concern."

She demurely lowered her lids. "Thank you."

They drank their tea in silence.

"I think I'll make a fire in the fireplace," he said abruptly, standing up.

"Whatever you say, Bill," Katie said, picturing a cozy scene in front of a cheerful fire, reading a Dr. Seuss book to their daughter.

He picked up his dishes. "I'll clean the table. You go relax. Later we'll go over the list, if it makes you feel better. If there's anything you want to add, you can."

"All right," she said, somehow managing not to grin. "I'll go up and take a bath." At the door, she paused. "I know you love marshmallows. There's a bag in the freezer. We'll toast a few later, okay?"

She scooted up the stairs into her room and let out a gurgle of laughter. Wait! she thought gleefully. She poured scented bubble bath into the tub, filled it with water, and stepped in. She sighed and closed her eyes and waited.

She didn't have to wait long.

"Katie!" Bill's voice thundered up the stairwell. Ah, yes, she thought. Music to her ears. "Katie, get down here."

Katie sponged herself. A few minutes passed. She heard Bill storm up the stairs.

"Katie!"

"What's the matter?" she trilled, pretending he hadn't yelled at her, but merely raised his voice to ask a question. "Weren't you able to find the marshmallows?"

"The hell with the damn marshmallows. Get out of that tub at once."

"I'm not finished."

"You've got two minutes!"

She giggled. And stayed put. For two minutes.

"I'm warning you."

She snuggled down in the steamy, soothing water.

"Last chance, Katie!"

She closed her eyes. Don't panic, she told herself, but she had never been so scared. Her insides were in turmoil, yet she was determined to brazen it out. This was the man she wanted for the rest of her life. It wasn't a trivial thing, but not even for Bill would she sacrifice herself. Her heart and soul were his for the taking—and no less. No compromises. She wouldn't, couldn't conceive a child for an instant divorce! Her fingers curled nervously around the sponge.

Bill barged in. "What's the meaning of this?"

Meeting his eyes unflinchingly, Katie sat up. She bent her knee, hiding from him that most private part of herself. Water slid down her shoulders, uncovering her shimmering nakedness. Small bubbles of soap slid down and around her breasts; several clung to her nipples like tiny pearls. Wispy tendrils of hair framed her face.

Bill stopped dead still. His breath was suddenly suspended. He gazed down the length of her body, and his eyes heated with desire. An eternity passed as neither said a word.

"You don't play fair, Katie," he said hoarsely.

She gestured toward the towel. "I thought you'd stay outside when you saw the closed door. You shouldn't be in here. Please go. I'll join you downstairs shortly."

Coming out of his trance, he held up her list of demands. His gaze slowly roved her naked body. "There's no way in hell I'm going to keep my hands off you once we're married, Katie. Especially now." He whirled and slammed the door shut behind him.

Although Bill couldn't know it, Katie had just given the performance of her life. She did not get up immediately. The water had chilled around her before she finally trusted her shaking limbs enough to step from the tub.

Bill splashed cold water on his face. Thinking of Katie in her bath brought a sheen of perspiration back, and he wiped his face again. This was his Katie, the girl he had known all his life. He'd always been able to talk sensibly with her. So what had he done? He'd barged into her bathroom, destroying her privacy, and in the process had gotten a good look at the goods he hadn't been given permission to touch, let alone kiss!

Desire shot through him as he remembered how she looked, her eyes startled and wide, her skin glistening and soft, her hair framing her face. He had wanted to pull her out of the tub and lick every drop of water off her luscious body.

Groaning, he stomped from the kitchen into the living room, then stood staring at the fire, trying to get himself under control. When he heard her light footsteps behind him, he spun around.

"I take it," Katie said as she swept into the room, "you object to the list."

# *Five*

---

Bill couldn't believe how cool she was. Covered from head to foot in an old chenille robe, she acted as if he hadn't seen her voluptuous body, as if she regularly held court for men while bathing. She wasn't the Katie he knew. The old Katie would scream bloody murder if a boy so much as tried pulling down her bathing suit's shoulder strap. The old Katie would have bashed the offender's head with a baseball bat, then followed it with a swift kick.

He felt blood rush through his veins like a locomotive out of control. How dare Miss Serenity parade into the room now, carrying her air of infuriating haughtiness! There wasn't a hint of reciprocal interest coming from her that he could discern. For all he knew, her mind was a million miles away, rather than on their important negotiations.

He needed precious little encouragement to answer her question. "You bet I object. Would you care to read these pearls of wisdom or shall I?"

Katie shrugged and pulled her copy of her rules

from her robe pocket. Settling herself on the couch near the fireplace, she tucked her feet under her and adjusted the ratty robe around her naked body.

"All right, Bill. We'll go over the list point by point."

"Start!" Positioning himself in a chair opposite her, he indicated with a nod that she read.

"Very well. The first rule is self-explanatory. I expect you to treat me with respect."

He handed her a pencil, keeping one for himself. "Granted. I require the same from you. Check it off. Next."

"I expect you to help with the housework."

"Fine. You wash, I'll wipe. Check it off. Next."

"I have a dishwasher," she said. "I was referring to your carrying the heavy bundles from the car into the house."

He fixed her with a righteous glare. "I'd hardly expect a pregnant woman to lift heavy bundles. Of course I'd do that. Check it off."

She smiled, then a look of distress crossed her face. "But when my pregnancy is advanced, if you're out of town—"

"I'll be here. Check it off."

"That's right, of course. We'll be going through Lamaze training. Write that down, I forgot."

The sounds of pencils racing across paper filled the air.

"It really is easy to come to terms, isn't it?" Katie said blithely, then went on to the next rule. "If we should argue—"

"Which we will," he assured her. "In about two rules from now."

She gave him a warning look. "We should discuss any infraction, major or minor, until we reach an agreement."

"All right, I agree. We'll talk until we're blue in the face, or until one of us runs out of breath. Check it off. Read the next rule."

She put down her list. "I'd like to explain about the previous rule. I wrote it so we wouldn't argue in front of our daughter. It's not a good idea for her to hear her parents argue."

"Son. And," he added, raising his voice, "that son will never happen unless you strike the next rule. I strongly object to the sleeping arrangements."

"Why?" she asked in sham innocence.

"Abstinence, your highness, is out!"

"Until we're married," she said calmly. "Do sit, Bill. Your pacing is giving me a crick in my neck. Oh, and do check off that rule."

A murderous expression flashed across his face. "The rule stinks. I prefer sleeping with a warm body next to mine, all night, every night."

"Do you always?" she asked, putting the right touch of amazement into her voice.

"Considering our objective, it's imperative."

"You mean you intend to do it more than once a night?"

"*It*, as you euphemistically call sex, can be done as often as two people wish, providing they're within touching distance and have the energy."

She sighed, capitulating. "We'll try it your way in the beginning. If it doesn't work out, you'll sleep in the spare room. Next rule."

Bill jerked his gaze from the list to her. "Wait a minute. What do you mean, 'If it doesn't work out'?"

She looked down at her hands. Her heart was fluttering like the wings of a trapped bird. "You know," she mumbled. "Energy."

He threw back his head and laughed. "Trust me, it'll work out," he said in amused exasperation.

"How can you be certain?"

"Shall I take you upstairs right now and prove it?"

She fixed him with a haughty glare but had to bite her lip to hide her smile. "That's not necessary."

"Too bad. Now then, I have a stipulation of my own."

His speculative scowl unnerved her. He began pacing again. Suddenly he stopped in front of her, sweeping his gaze up from her bare toes to her face, lingering at her breasts on the way.

"Which is?" she prodded, feeling as if he'd undressed her.

"You are not to claim a convenient headache."

"But what if I really have one?" she protested.

He grinned. "Believe me, I know exactly how to relax you. Write down my rule, then check it off."

"This is preposterous!"

"Agreed," he said, nonplussed. "Let's tear up the damn list. It's idiotic."

He'd neatly cornered her and they both knew it.

"Sign your copy," she said. "I'll sign mine. But let me warn you. Right now I don't like you very much. Perhaps other women appreciate cave man tactics. I don't. I prefer men who are gentle, who are gentlemen in every sense of the word. Men who notice me with my clothes on, thank you, not the way you've been undressing me with your eyes. Men who appreciate my brain too. Men who don't make me feel as if I'm being evaluated for my breeding ability like some cow or horse! You seem to have forgotten your roots. It's a pity. It really is. Frankly, I'm not so sure I care to go through with this."

"Katie," he said succinctly, "we are getting married. I did not sign this thing for my health. I am going to be a father."

Silence.

"If I fall in love with you," she added, stalling for the time she needed to change his attitude.

"Love?" he hooted. "Since when did love enter our deal? We agreed to this arrangement, rule by silly rule."

She elaborately rearranged her robe. Using the warmth from the fire as an excuse, she unbuttoned the top three buttons, slowly folding back the neckline to display an enticing cleavage.

"I agreed on certain conditions," she said, lifting her hair away from her neck. "Those conditions are noted in the list."

"Then we're saying the same thing, aren't we?"

"Not exactly. I'm glad I entice you. I'm glad my body makes yours—how shall I delicately phrase it?—spring to life. However, that's a physical response, a conditioned reflex. Pavlov did it with dogs. In your case, you happened to see me naked."

"Are you saying I got hard because of a conditioned reflex?" He bellowed.

Katie's elegant nostrils quivered. "Precisely." She glanced down, as if too embarrassed to continue. "Bill, I wish I had the same reaction toward you. Unfortunately, I didn't. I am, as you"—she coughed—"as you have already seen, constructed differently. On a certain level, love to a man—to you—is nothing. To me, and to most women, love—the perception of love—is essential. A man reacts mechanically to the sex act. A woman needs . . . handling."

He glared at her. "How the hell do you know so much? What have you been doing all these years?"

She favored him with a censorious look that spoke volumes but gave away nothing.

"Don't be insulting, Bill. This isn't easy for me. As I was saying, foreplay—followed by the male's participation in copulation—"

"Katie! For Pete's sake!"

"Bill," she continued, although the stress accumulating in her neck was beginning to give her a headache, "to get through the act, I have to at least pretend to love you. Even with the rule about sleeping together all night long, it's not going to be easy for me to fantasize. I hardly know you any more. Don't get me wrong. I'm not trying to insult you. You look more or less the same. You're as handsome as you ever were. You're not fat or ugly, but I'm going to need your help. Lots of it. I need arousing, stroking, kissing, whispered love words. It's the least you can do for me. I already told you, I first have to like you before we marry—for longer than forty-eight hours."

Bill made a choked sound.

She went on. "Barging into my bathroom while I was in the tub didn't help your cause. You can't deny you're displeased about waiting until we're married to have sex. I seriously doubt if waiting a few days after we're married to consummate the act will tax you. Call it a rehearsal. I'm willing to share your bed. I'll allow you—even insist—you hold me and fondle me, but you cannot force me to let you join your body with mine. It's up to you to make me feel loved. Very loved. Don't forget, I know why you're doing it."

She looked up at him, smiling benignly. "In short, Bill, your job is to get me in the mood to fantasize my way through this. My job, the hard job, comes later. For nine long months."

He cursed. Explicit words singed her ears. From his expression, she guessed Bill had a distinctly vivid picture of joining his body with hers, and the sooner it happened, the sooner he'd like it.

Katie wanted to hug herself.

"Calm down, Bill. Between kissing Janice today and taking over my home, you're falling short of the mark."

He slammed his fist against his open palm.

Her eyes widened. "Unless you prefer calling the whole thing off?"

Bill studied her pouty mouth and innocent eyes and remembered her naked. He also remembered how quickly she had aroused him. If only she didn't talk so damn much! "You want me to make you fall in love with me—"

"Temporarily," she clarified. "To do the task."

He cut her off coldly and decisively. "Sons," he said coldly, "are not *tasks*. A son is a precious human being—"

"Conceived in love." She waved her hand dismissively, as if adding, "Blah, blah, blah" to his speech. "A daughter conceived, I hope, by parents who will bring her into this world with the best intentions."

"I refuse to argue the sex of the child with you. It's ridiculous. However, I'm certain it will be a boy."

"Now this is important. Are you saying if you have a daughter, you won't love her?"

Absolute bafflement came over his face. "Of course I would. Girls are—"

"Cute and cuddly and they wrap their fathers around their chubby little fingers. Perhaps I would like a son, after all."

"Now that you describe her, a girl would be welcome. And I'd like to remind her mother that there's still the matter of creation."

Katie lifted the paper to hide her face. "You're tired. Go back to the hotel and reread the rules, then get some sleep. We'll discuss this again tomorrow when you're in a more reasonable frame of mind. Good night, Bill."

"Not so fast." He snatched her list of rules away and thrust his face close to hers. Her perfume wafted into his nostrils, knocking him in the solar plexus like a one-two punch. "First we settle this, then we destroy the list, then you go to bed. Speaking of beds, if you think I'm going to hold you and fondle you and not, as you graphically describe, join my body with yours, you're really nuts."

She looked disappointed. "That's precisely what I expect. You've missed the point."

"Point, hell! Listen to me, Miss Teacher. Grow up. Let me give you a few male realities. You are not going to get me hot and bothered the way you did upstairs, or even now, you rotten minx. No way! When the time comes, I'm going to slowly kiss your clothes off your tempting body. Next I'm going to kiss you all over without clothes on. In other words, *naked*. From your toes to your head and down again. With some pretty nice stops along the way. You'll love it, I promise you. When you're writhing in my arms, I'm going to bury myself inside you. Hard and full and deep. If you don't like it, you can sleep through it!"

She thought it sounded heavenly, but she shot him a hostile look. "That's it," she announced, pushing herself up off the couch. "Separate rooms for the first three days after marriage. You leave me no choice. You're far too animalistic. If this is how you think now, when we haven't kissed, except to make up and we agreed that doesn't count, or dated or petted—Well! I'll have to adjust my plans. I can imagine what a primitive you'd be if we shared a bed right away."

She clutched her chest as if to protect herself. "You'd have your hands all over me while I, on the other hand, tried my sincere best—for old time's sake—to adjust to the mere idea of being married. Bill, forget the baby. Tear up the list. Call Sy. Tell him to stay home. Oh, and good luck with your knees."

She almost made it past him. Then his lips were on hers so fast, she didn't know what hit her. He literally stormed the gates, parting her lips with his tongue. She gasped her surprise, giving him entry, and he rapaciously took advantage. His hand moved to her breast and cupped it. Pushing aside her robe, he raked his thumb across the nipple. With his other hand at her back, he pressed her against him, bringing her into steaming contact with his frustration and need. He sent her senses reeling, scalding her with a kiss and caresses that were anything but gentle.

Katie tore her lips from his and thumped both hands on his chest. Their gazes clashed. She won. "You've just proven my point."

He took one step back. "You are the most exasperating woman I know."

Katie breathed a sigh of relief. At least *she,* not the baby, had gotten his attention. Another minute and she would have dragged him down to the floor. "Cheer up. We finally understand each other. Agreed?" His face had grown so thoughtful, she feared he was ready to call the whole thing off.

"Agreed," he said after a long pause. "I'm sorry I was rough with you."

And that was another small step for her, she thought. "We should make a terrific daughter. She's bound to be the most stubborn kid in the world. I wonder what other traits she'll have."

"Son," he said, his voice a husky promise. His hooded gaze held more than desire. As he closed her robe, she wanted to tell him that she knew she had caused his anger, but she didn't. She wanted to lay her hands on his chest, but she didn't. She wanted to stroke his cheeks, to push his hair away from his forehead, to kiss him gently, to hold his head to her breast, but she didn't. Not yet.

Too much was at stake. Being good old agreeable Katie wasn't enough. She fumbled with her belt, then drew the courage to raise her eyes. Their gazes clung, and she felt her resolve crumble. She had played a dangerous game, unfairly goading Bill.

"Perhaps we both owe each other an apology," she said. "It isn't wise for us to remember a kiss taken in anger."

"No," he said softly. "It isn't."

Gazing at her face, Bill felt something far more exciting than any sensation he'd ever known. She was so fine, so infinitely desirable. Her eyes were deep and green, her mouth enticing. He'd come very close to losing her. A fact, he realized, that bothered him more than anything else. They'd been arguing over a baby, yet all the time, he'd been thinking of her.

Katie didn't miss the expression of wonder that crossed Bill's face, and her heart pounded hard in her chest. "Then if you please," she said, her voice slightly unsteady, "I'd like you to kiss me now. We can suspend our three-day moratorium due to the unusual circumstances."

"You're sure?" he asked, and she saw a gleam of amusement in his eyes.

"I'm sure. I'm trying. I would say we're past the shy stage," she added boldly, finding a glimmer of humor to match his.

His speculative glance strayed to her bosom, and he thought of how her breast had swelled to fit his palm. His hand tangled in her hair. He brought his lips to her forehead, murmuring, "I would say so, Katie."

They came together with lips and hands that stroked as gently as a soft spring rain. Her hair shone with golden highlights. His glinted with the sheen of reflected firelight. Her lips were soft.

His firm. His hand crept up to her throat, bringing her close. It ended as gently as it had begun.

At precisely eight the next morning, Katie unlocked Sweet Mischief's front door. She was amazed she wasn't late. Having skipped breakfast in favor of a long walk on the boardwalk, she'd lost track of the time and had to hurry home to shower and dress. The night before, after Bill had left, she'd lain on the sofa, staring at the shadowed wall and wishing Bill were there. With only the kitten for company, she'd tried to recall her earliest memories of him. Was it the time he pulled her out of a mud hole, or was it the day she dragged him to her house to see a frog she'd captured and put in a box? Or was it her first day of school, when he shoved her to the head of the kindergarten line and then went off to find his classmates?

"Am I interrupting?"

Katie looked up to see Sally's husband, Eric, standing at the door to her office. She'd known and liked Eric since the seventh grade. She had ordered her new carpeting from his store.

"Not at all," she said. "I was woolgathering."

"I'm glad you changed your mind and decided on the upgrade for the carpeting. Bill asked if we could install it Sunday so you won't lose business. I wanted to check with you if this Sunday's all right."

Startled, she asked, "When did you see Bill?"

"A little while ago. It was like old times. Jimmy, Pete, and Ben were there too. We all had coffee over at Grannie's Kitchen. We all think Bill's news is wonderful."

"What news?" She motioned for him to sit in the other chair.

"Why, that he's moving back. I guess you already know all that, seeing as how he's renting a room at your place."

She nearly had a stroke. Eric took her silence as permission to gab. "Bill explained it. If you ask me, it makes good sense. What with his restoring your house and all."

"And all?" She picked up a pencil and nearly broke it. "What else did he tell you?"

Eric tapped his fingers on his leg. "He said you're planning a wingding of a party at your place once the house is in shape."

After several horrified seconds, she asked, "Anything else?"

"No, not unless you count his talking about buying the house next door to yours. Well." He slapped his palms on his thighs. "I better go. See you and Bill on Sunday."

Katie hit the floor running the moment Eric left. So this was the way Bill apologized! He might as well have taken an ad out in the local paper. By nightfall every one of the old gang would know where to find him—living with her!

She slid behind the wheel of her car and gunned the motor. "Don't you dare give out on me now!"

Three blocks later she came to her senses. She reversed her direction, returned to the store, and filled Phyllis in on the latest.

"Katie, you almost blew it again," Phyllis said. "It's time to step up our campaign."

"*Our* campaign?"

Phyllis opened her purse and took from it a picture of a dress she had cut from a magazine. She handed it to Katie. "I've got a vested interest in this. Besides, you need all the help you can get. Without me to guide you, your thinking's too clouded."

"I can't wear this! It's not me."

"You can and it will be," Phyllis insisted. "If it's your intention to get morning sickness, a protruding belly, and swollen ankles, go buy the dress."

"It's not a dress. It's a towel with sequins. It's so tight, I won't be able to sit down. It's too short. If I'm lucky the bodice might cover my breasts. No." She handed back the picture.

Phyllis refused to take it. "And don't forget to buy a black garter belt," she said. "Also some baby oil."

Katie stared at the picture. "Where am I going to wear this? It's so planned. It doesn't seem right."

"You want to play fair, think of Janice."

"You're right. I left my credit card at home. I'm going to get it."

Katie found Bill at the house, clad in jeans and work boots, inspecting the foundation. A ladder lay on the lawn. The kitten scampered near his feet. Around his waist, he wore a cobbler's apron. He looked so appealing, so sexy, she had to remind herself not to throw herself in his arms.

He shaded his eyes with his hand. " 'Morning, Katie. What's up?"

She halted at the edge of the path, and for a breathtaking moment their gazes spoke of the previous night's emotion. Then Bill looked down to rewind his tape measure. "Did Eric stop by the store? Is Sunday okay?"

Regardless of Phyllis's advice, Katie was still her own person. "I saw Eric."

"And?"

"Bill, haven't you any idea how this will get around?"

"There's no law against working on Sunday. I figured you didn't want to disrupt the store when people are shopping. You're closed on Sunday."

"You might have told me."

"I didn't think you'd mind," he drawled.

"About buying the house next door."

"Oh, that." He stepped toward her and caught her hand. "Let's go inside," he said urgently. "Get your copy of the rules."

"Now?"

"Right now," he ordered. "There's something I want to add to it."

She fetched it from the living room and thrust it at him. "Here."

He scribbled a word on the bottom and gave it back to her. "Read it."

She did. *Trust.*

She looked at him sheepishly but decided to argue for just a moment more. "I still don't like you announcing to the whole world you're living in my house. Why didn't you tell me about your intention to buy the place next door?"

"You knew I planned to move back after the baby was born. Anyway, you didn't give me a chance last night. I'm going to need a place to run my business. There's no industry involved, so

I won't be breaking any zoning laws. I've already checked at city hall."

That gave Katie an idea. "I suppose it's a good thing you're buying it," she said. "You can baby-sit when I date."

He grabbed her arm. "Who said anything about your dating? I'm not planning on dating. How can you talk about that now?"

She patted his cheek. "Bill darling, be reasonable. Of course you will. So will I. Naturally, after the baby is born, I expect to resume my private life. There's a marvelous yard next door with room for swings and slides. Who better than our daughter's father to baby-sit?"

He drew in a deep breath. "I don't know anything about babies." Even if he did, he didn't like the idea of her with another man. She had him moving out before he moved in.

He had spent a pleasurable hour picturing them sharing their baby's growth, discovering each fascinating step of his progress. He wanted to watch Katie breast-feed their son. He most assuredly did not intend to baby-sit so that she could date!

"What happens if he's hungry?" he demanded.

"That's a silly question. You'll feed her."

"How?" he growled. "Aren't you planning to breast-feed him?"

Heat rose up in her. "My goodness! You are getting ahead of yourself. Of course I'll breast-feed our daughter."

"Not," he said implacably, "if you're out on a date."

She smiled. She enjoyed his jealousy. Another

small step for Katie. "When I date, I'll pump my breasts."

He frowned. They gazed at each other in silence for a moment, then he said suddenly, "Katie, I have an idea. Let's get away for the weekend. You said you wanted a courtship. We can go to Atlantic City and break the bank, dance, have fun. Would you like that?"

She didn't want to appear too happy. "Eric. What about Eric and the carpet?"

"We'll leave a key with Phyllis. Come on, Katie. We're both uptight. Let's get away. We could both use some fun."

The kitten padded in and played between their legs. "We can't leave Samson," she said.

"We'll look in the phone book for a cat-sitter."

"Your foreman is coming today."

"I called Sy late last night. He's coming in on Monday instead. After what happened, I figured we needed time alone."

He draped his long arms over her shoulders, rubbing noses with her. He smelled of the outdoors, a clean, male smell.

"Will you come?" he asked. "You can bring your bathing suit and we'll swim in the pool. I'll race you and maybe I'll let you beat me. Katie, I didn't return to make you unhappy. Please believe me."

"I know," she said, dropping her pose. "I want you to be happy too. It's just that everything is happening so fast. What do you think our folks would say if they knew this?"

His mouth turned down. "There's no need to tell them, is there?"

"I'd prefer not to. Mom would want a big wedding with all the trimmings." She sighed, and he felt her tremble. "I guess when we're ready we'd better elope. If there's no baby they won't need to know we were married. We can have a quiet divorce."

"Whatever you say." He sounded less cheerful. The idea of Katie wanting to end the marriage as much as he did wasn't as appealing as he had first thought.

Unaware of his perplexed feelings, Katie said, "First things first. We're getting way ahead of ourselves. I've got some shopping to do. When would you like to leave for Atlantic City?"

"How about later this afternoon?"

"Great. It's time to get on with our courtship."

# Six

Bill zipped up his overnight bag. Although he was glad he'd talked Katie into going away with him for the weekend, he felt despondent. Being back in the picturesque community where he could let his gaze wander over the architectural beauty of nineteenth-century houses wasn't fun if he was causing Katie's unhappiness. He'd be a fool if he didn't know he was putting her under pressure, yet he also knew she wanted the baby too. She'd looked adorable that morning in her white wool coat with the collar turned up to frame her face. While he had been dying to nuzzle her neck and find out whether she smelled of flowers as she had after her bath, she hit him between the eyes with the baby-sitter business! They hadn't made love, hadn't married, hadn't gotten pregnant, hadn't gotten divorced, and all she could think of was dating other men! In a little while he'd pick her up for the thirty-five mile drive to Atlantic City, where, he hoped, he'd put her in a more amiable frame of mind.

Katie had grown into a fine woman, which

didn't surprise him. She'd always been talented and had always encouraged and supported others. From his earliest memory of her, her sense of humor had drawn him to her. He sighed and braced his temple on a finger. His Katie had become one strong-minded lady. It hadn't always been the case.

He remembered the first time he'd seen Katie cry. She was four years old. Her frog had died, and she insisted on a formal funeral. Her mother found a shoe box, and her dad put the frog in newspaper before setting it in the box. Sobbing, Katie ran to his house, tearing him away from building a fort out of scraps of wood his father had given him. One look at her face and he knew it was serious. She clenched his hand and, through her gulps, asked him to officiate.

Embarrassed with her parents listening, he mumbled a few words that passed for a prayer. Her dad lowered the shoe box into the dirt, patted her head, and left them alone. Her mother asked if they wanted milk and cookies. He was dying for some. Katie, in the throes of misery, refused. He remembered being grateful none of his friends witnessed what happened next. Katie sat on the grass beneath the weeping willow tree. She tugged him down beside her, then crawled into his lap and cried for her dead frog. Desperately casting about for a way to make her stop bawling, he promised her the frog wasn't stiff and cold, but jumping around in frog heaven in another frog's body.

Katie gradually stopped crying and fell asleep. He plucked blades of grass, scared to move lest he awaken her and she'd start drenching his shirt again. To his surprise and delight, when she woke, she was smiling. She told him the frog was fine, just like he'd promised. She had seen the frog in her dreams, jumping around in another frog's body.

Bill shook his head. Funny he should think of Katie's frog now.

Back then Katie had treated him as if she owned him—along with her stuffed animals. During her grammar-school days, he'd known which friend was her current best, which book she liked the most, which food her mother made her eat that she hated—broccoli topped the list—and which teacher she liked the best.

Phyllis moved to town when Katie was in the fourth grade. The two rapidly became thick as thieves. Apparently they still were. A lot had happened since they'd grown up. He was successful in business. Katie was struggling to make a success of Sweet Mischief. Phyllis was married with a second child on the way. She held the key to happiness. Happiness, he'd learned, came in different forms. He'd meant it when he told Katie that he wished he could fall in love for the long haul.

Bill stared out the window at the ocean. A sailboat passed, its colorful sails billowing in the wind. People strolled the boardwalk, enjoying the sunshine. The ocean and the boardwalk were part of his fondest memories. He and Katie used to sit on a bench and pull taffy to see who ended up with the largest piece. Or they would frolic in the water after their endurance swim. Once she swam out too far, refusing to come back as he ordered. He had gone in after her. They'd had a hell of a row. She had been a moody thirteen-year-old then. After that he began seeing her less, except in groups. His main interest, aside from sports and working with his dad, was girls, not Katie's teasing him about wearing cologne.

Bill thrust his hands deep in his pockets. He had taken a lot for granted, including Katie. Her question about how their parents would react to their arrangement had set him thinking. His folks loved her, she'd been part of his family. They'd understand. He had no idea how her parents would view it, but he knew it bothered Katie. Her mother and father were getting on in years. Thinking it all through, he was glad he hadn't argued when Katie insisted on their marrying. She was finer, more beautiful than anyone he knew, and deserved to be treated with respect.

Suddenly he scowled, remembering what she'd said about dating. He detested the idea of her kissing another man the way she had kissed him, because now he knew *exactly* what it felt like to experience the sweet ecstasy of her drugging kisses.

Katie removed a box of nougats from the shelf and dropped it and a box of taffy into her shopping bag. "For Bill's sweet tooth," she told Phyllis. "Sally's coming in tomorrow. It will be a good time to train her, don't you think?"

With her elbows resting on the counter, Phyllis stifled a yawn. "Yes, I do. Charlie has a cold. He kept me up last night. And so did this little guy. Did you buy the dress?"

Katie nodded.

"Then why aren't you more excited? I'd be."

"Oh, Phil. This isn't a game I'm trying to win. This is my life. It's Bill's too." She arranged a tray of chocolate logs. "There's more. I told you Bill is thinking of buying the house next door to mine for his business."

"It makes sense."

Katie came around the counter. "I'm afraid, despite your warning, I wasn't very nice to him about it. I told him he could baby-sit our daughter while I date. He didn't appreciate that."

Phyllis laughed. "I should hope not. You must be driving him crazy. He talks son, you talk daughter."

"If I am driving him crazy, it's mutual. I'm making this up as I go along, you know."

Phyllis dropped down into the chair she'd set beside the cash register. "Remind yourself why you're doing this. And while you're at it, don't be upset about Bill giving Eric permission to upgrade the carpet. Eric doesn't know it didn't come from you. Bill is being generous."

Katie whipped around. "He expects payment, don't forget that."

"But you intend on going through with this. When the time comes, I mean."

Katie shrugged. "I don't know, Phil. One minute I think I will, the next I'm mixed up. There are moments when I'm sure Bill wants me for myself. Then it feels right. Otherwise it doesn't."

"But you're making progress."

Katie deflated. "At what cost?"

"Forget the cost," Phyllis advised. "Ask yourself if Bill is worth it. You're the only one capable of making that decision."

Katie fixed a troubled gaze on her friend. It seemed to her that what she was doing to Bill was wrong. She didn't want to enjoy herself at his expense, or to trick him. He treated her honestly. He'd been up-front with her, stating his intentions from the outset.

A slow flush crept up her neck and stained her cheeks. She thought of Bill holding her and kissing her, of all the outrageous things she'd told him. He wasn't a boy. All traces of his youth had left him. He wasn't someone she could wrap around her little finger. Last night he'd frightened her, yet also excited her. She had witnessed his struggle to contain his temper after she told him she needed to fantasize to get through the sex act. Had she teased him too unfairly?

In her mind's eye she saw him waving to her that morning as she got out of her car, a cocky grin on his face—until she'd wiped it off.

"Bill's worth it, Phyllis. I never realized how much."

"Then don't let me hear this nonsense again."

Katie stopped at the beauty salon on the way home to buy shampoo and conditioner. Glenda Lewes owned and operated the salon. A woman in her forties, she had lived in Cape May all her life.

"I hear Bill's back," she said, ringing up Katie's purchase. Katie pretended not to hear her. "Rumor has it he's here to stay."

"Who told you?" Katie asked, unable to resist.

"Janice did. She came in this morning for her weekly appointment. She was very perky. Girl's got that look in her eye again. I understand Bill's renting a room at your place."

Katie's forehead puckered. "His foreman will be there, too, once the restoration work begins. Did Janice tell you about Bill staying at my house?"

"No, Eric told my husband."

Glenda talked on for several more minutes. Her conversation ranged from ways to attract more winter customers from the neighboring towns to the latest hairstyles, then back to Janice's success with men.

Katie cut short the conversation. "Glenda, if you hear more gossip, be sure to tell me."

Katie continued on toward home, though the heavy traffic made it slow going. An unusual number of conventions were in town. As they were good for business, she didn't mind the traffic. When she stopped for a red light, her thoughts wandered to Janice. How did she know Bill's plans? Before jealousy reared its ugly head again, Katie reminded herself that Janice knew because of small-town gossip. Eric told Sally. Sally told Janice. Glenda told everybody.

Katie pulled up in front of her house and turned off the engine. She had her house key in the lock when she heard the clanging of the phone. She rushed into the kitchen. "Hello," she said.

"Hello," Bill said. She smiled at the sound of his voice. "Ready to go?"

She unbuttoned her coat. "Give me half an hour, okay?"

"Okay. Katie . . ."

Samson purred. Katie shushed him. "No, not you, Bill. The kitten's on my shoe. His motor's going. Speak up."

# The Publisher of Loveswept® Romances invites you to:

## CLAIM A FREE EXCLUSIVE ROMANCE

Lift Here

## ...PLUS SIX ROMANCES RISK FREE

**6 ROMANCES FREE**

Detach and affix this stamp to the postage-paid reply card and mail at once!

## NO OBLIGATION TO BUY!

## THE FREE GIFT IS YOURS TO KEEP

**SEE DETAILS INSIDE ▶**

# LET YOURSELF BE LOVESWEPT BY...
# SIX BRAND NEW
# LOVESWEPT ROMANCES!

*Because Loveswept romances sell themselves ...we want to send you six (Yes, six!) exciting new novels to enjoy for 15 days — risk free! — without obligation to buy.*

Discover how these compelling stories of contemporary romances tug at your heart strings and keep you turning the pages. Meet true-to-life characters you'll fall in love with as their romances blossom. Experience their challenges and triumphs — their laughter, tears and passion.

**Let yourself be Loveswept!** Join our **at-home reader service!** Each month we'll send you six new Loveswept novels **before they appear in the bookstores.** Take up to **15 days to preview** current selections **risk-free! Keep only those shipments you want.** Each book is yours for only $2.09 plus postage & handling, and sales tax where applicable — **a savings of 41¢ per book** off the cover price.

# NO OBLIGATION TO BUY — WITH THIS RISK-FREE OFFER!

Bill laughed, and she pictured the corners of his eyes crinkling. "This better?"

"Yes," she said.

Silence.

"Are you still there, Bill?"

"I'm here."

"Bill, is everything okay?"

Silence.

"Bill, are you all right?"

"I'm fine."

He didn't sound it. "Bill, what is it?"

"I just wanted to tell you not to worry, Katie. I got to thinking today."

The house was cool, but she was suddenly hot. "About what?"

"Mostly the old days."

"Oh."

"Actually I was thinking about your frog."

"My frog?" He wasn't making sense.

"Yeah. I remembered it, out of the blue. You were four years old. It was August, and the day was hot as hell. Your frog died. You ran to get me. You wanted me to say a prayer for your frog. You tucked your hand in mine, Katie. After the funeral, you sat on my lap under the weeping willow tree and fell asleep. You had been crying, Katie."

Goose bumps rose on her arms. He remembered that!

"Katie?"

She pressed her fingertips to her lips. She was too choked up to speak.

"Katie, are you still there?"

"I'm here, Bill."

"Yeah, well . . . it's funny how things pop into your head, isn't it? I'll see you in a little while."

Katie very softly hung up the phone.

Atlantic City proved the perfect diversion. The town thrived on tourism, with flashing neon lights everywhere to attract customers. Huge hotels and casinos provided noise and distraction.

"Taste gives way to opulence, Katie," Bill said, gesturing at the garish decor of the lobby of their hotel. "Red, gold, and blinking lights."

Katie stared at a hostess in black fishnet stockings, spike heels, a miniskirt, and a blouse cut so low her breasts would surely fall out if she bent over. Katie laughed. "You're right. I love it."

He left her to sign in. When he returned after a few minutes he found Katie avidly watching a woman feed half dollars into a slot machine. His arm around her shoulders, he led her to the elevator, up to the sixth floor.

"Relax," he told her as he unlocked the door. "I booked two rooms."

Her nervousness gave way to giggles the moment she stepped across the threshold. The hedonistic bedroom could have been lifted from an illustration in the *Arabian Nights*. The round bed was enclosed in a tentlike structure. Its top and sides consisted of red-and-gold striped silken material, attached to the frame with gold tassels. Multicolored pillows were strewn across the head of the bed.

Bill whistled. "Bring on the dancing girls."

Katie leaned against the padded arm of the

sofa, still staring. "Can you imagine? Two people could hide in there and never be found."

"That's an idea," Bill said half teasingly. He put her case on a red velvet bench.

"You're right," she replied. "I should have brought Samson instead of leaving him with the sitter."

That earned a grunt from Bill. He didn't look content. When Katie suggested he go to his room so she could change for dinner, he gave every appearance of a man being sent to the dog house. His room was identical to hers except for the color of the material over the bed. He hauled his suitcase into his room, and she closed the door behind him.

"Bill." Katie knocked on the adjoining door about an hour later. "Would you mind? I need help."

He rushed in, only too happy to be out of his room and in hers.

Standing in front of the mirror over the dresser, Katie whipped her long hair over her head. As she turned her back to Bill, their gazes caught in the mirror. His eyes narrowed. His hand, lifting to draw her back for a kiss, froze in midair. There, propped against the edge of the mirror, was Katie's copy of the list of rules with his signature at the bottom.

"What did you bring that for?" he asked crossly. He wanted to take a match to the list and burn the damned thing.

She returned his gaze steadily. A shadow of a smile touched her mouth. Trapped by the irony of the situation, he noticed she looked lovely and vulnerable, with her glowing red hair framing her pretty face. her lips were parted and shiny from lipstick. She lowered her lashes. "It's merely a safety precaution."

"Some courtship!" he muttered.

"Please, darling," she said, "we've been all through this. We came here to have a good time. I'm having trouble releasing this pesky catch. The necklace doesn't go with my dress."

With shaking hands, he unclasped the necklace. Her perfume tempted him. "We'd better go," he said huskily, resisting the impulse to kiss her. He didn't want to leave, but Katie's list of rules flashed at him as surely as if it were on a neon sign!

Katie stepped back to give herself one final appraisal. She'd chosen to wear one of her two new dresses. Figuring she'd done all she could to further her cause for one night, she'd decided to save the blue sequin for the following night. Tonight she wore a black-and-white paisley silk and chiffon cocktail dress. Her only jewelry was onyx and faux diamond earrings.

She tucked her arm through his. Bill, dressed in a tailored dark gray suit, white shirt, and black tie, looked exceedingly handsome.

They wandered through the gaming rooms, ducked into a private room. When they learned the stakes were an astronomical one thousand dollars minimum, they came out shaking their heads.

"Were you tempted?" he asked.

She looked horrified. "Are you kidding? The quarter slots are more my style. If I lost big money, I'd die on the spot."

He grinned. "I forgot. You're the lady who shops mattress sales."

His comment made her think of the bed upstairs, large enough for a harem. Large enough to lose herself in Bill's arms.

"Hungry?" he asked.

She bobbed her head. "Starved. We don't have to eat here, Bill. We can go to one of the good restaurants away from the hotels. It's only a meal. These places gouge the tourist."

He studied her, thinking about how much he valued her friendship and how she was trying to help them both get past a sticky situation. He knew that in cases such as theirs, most women would be calculating, doing their best to take the man for all he was worth.

He smiled and brushed her jaw with his knuckles. "Don't worry about money, Katie. You look beautiful. I want to show you off."

His compliment sent a shiver through her. "I suppose I sound like a harpy about money, but it's second nature, Bill."

"Not this weekend. Fair enough, pretty lady?"

She smiled up at him. "Fair enough. Guess what?"

"What?"

"I brought you a present."

He grinned. "I bet I know what it is."

"How could you?"

"Five will get you ten, it's candy."

Her surprise was evident. She swatted him. "I hate it when you guess. You did that when we were kids, no matter what I bought you. All right, what kind?"

"Taffy. Saltwater taffy and nougats."

Her lower jaw dropped. "You cheated! You peeked in the car," she wailed in dismay.

He laughed. "Not only that, I sneaked a piece when I put our things in the car."

She fell weakly against his chest. He placed a finger under her chin, urging it up until she was looking at him. With their arms looped lightly around each other, they smiled. "You always were a lot of fun, squirt."

"Good old dependable Katie. Is that right?" she asked, starting to lose her good cheer.

"Most definitely. I always know where I stand with you."

"Dependable." She was coming to despise the word. "As in friends forever?"

"Of course. Best friends. Friends with a very special arrangement," he added, feeling genuinely annoyed. He was quite prepared to punch the lights out of the first man Katie tried to date!

"That's what I like about you, Bill. Except for your relapse when you barged into my bathroom, you're generally trustworthy. And you're right."

"About what?"

"From now on, I'm not going to worry about money. As you say, we have a special arrangement. You said we're here for fun, so I'm taking your suggestion. Let's have fun. I feel lucky. What do you say we try one of the tables? Afterward we'll catch the show. Then we'll hit the other spots."

"Whatever you say," he agreed.

She looked him straight in the eye. "I want to compliment you for not kissing me before."

"How about if we do everything but kiss?"

She playfully slapped his arm. "What a kidder you are. I'd forgotten your sense of humor."

That earned a scowl.

"I've become a fast learner over the years," she said.

He glanced down at her flushed face, her too-bright smile, and at her breasts, which were making enticing contact with his chest. He hoped she hadn't learned too much. There were a few things he wanted to teach her!

"We'll stay out all night and watch the sunrise," she added.

He'd much rather watch the sunrise with her from a bed, preferably in his room where he didn't have a copy of the rules!

# Seven

Katie was determined to have an evening to remember. After playing several rounds of roulette, they stuffed themselves with an exorbitant but delicious dinner, then went to hear Liza Minnelli sing. The maître d' seated them close to the stage at a long table, sandwiched between couples from Alabama and Ohio. It was worth it. The show was wonderful. Liza Minnelli sang a song to Bill, who took it in stride. The lyrics were filled with tantalizing suggestions. When the song ended, he whispered in Katie's ear, "Why don't we do what she said?"

Katie gulped. She was quaking inside. After several mute seconds, she said, "Think of the baby."

He placed a soft kiss on her lips. "I am. Believe me, I am."

She shuddered involuntarily. Every part of her wanted to surrender. Like a woman condemned by her own words, though, she resolved to stick to her guns. The show soon ended, and she was surprised when Bill nixed the idea of returning to the gaming rooms. "I'd rather dance, Katie."

She readily agreed. On the small, crowded dance floor, she laid her head on his chest and closed her eyes. His hand was warm on her spine and he moved like a dream. How could this hurt? she wondered. No subterfuge, no snappy repartee. She pretended Bill was madly in love with her.

Later he suggested having dessert, which both had declined at dinner. They found a brightly lit coffee shop, and seated side by side in a booth, they shared a sinfully delicious chocolate fudge brownie with vanilla ice cream.

"One minute," he said, cupping her chin. "You've got a little chocolate by the side of your mouth." She started to reach for her napkin. "I've got a better idea." He brought his lips to hers and with a flick of his tongue, licked the chocolate off. Her resolve slipped several more notches.

Katie put down her spoon. "What would you like to do now, Bill?"

The question hung like a heavy pall. Seconds passed. At last he said, "Let's take a walk. Wait here, I'll get our coats."

Outside they strolled hand in hand along the boardwalk. The beach was empty save for a few hardy youths around a campfire. After fifteen minutes they sat down on a bench to watch the moon shimmering on the ocean. Bill propped his feet up on the railing in front of them.

"Have you missed living near the water?" she asked.

"A little," he said, brushing a strand of hair

from her cheek. "I've been on the go so much. Being here makes me realize how much I miss it."

"Won't it be difficult to give up your home?" He had described his sprawling three-bedroom ranch in California, with the pool and cabana on two acres of land.

He flashed an unrepentant grin. "No. I've decided to keep it until we see how things go."

That remark went to the bone. "You never give up, do you?"

"You asked."

"Let's walk."

They did. Up and down the boardwalk while Katie let off steam and Bill used the time to get a brilliant idea.

"This," he said through chattering teeth, "is fun." He blew into his hands, slapping them several times. His chattering increased. He stopped to do a few jumping jacks. He slapped his hands together again. He shook violently.

"What's wrong?" Katie asked, concerned.

He rubbed his hands on his arms. "Nothing. I'm a little cold."

"We'd better go back. A nice cup of tea will do you good."

He hated tea. "And ruin your good time? Don't be silly." He tucked his hands into his pockets. "If we walk faster, I'll be fine."

"This is ridiculous. Bill, it's not worth getting sick."

He sniffled. "Katie, stop worrying. I'm fine."

"Don't be stubborn. You're not fine. Look at you. I insist we go back."

He tucked his chin on his chest, shivering

effectively. "Katie, I'm determined to give you a good time this weekend. Getting sick isn't on the agenda. I'm a big man. This'll pass."

"Big men get sick too," she stated. "Don't be a hero."

He gave her a woeful look and briskly rubbed his hands on his arms. "You don't mind?"

"I suggested it, didn't I? When did you first feel chilled?" she asked, reversing their direction and hurrying him along. "You were fine a little while ago."

He thought fast. "I know. It's the strangest thing, now that I think about it. I felt chilled this morning, then it passed. Now I'm freezing."

'I'm getting you to bed," she announced.

*Amen.* "You really don't mind?"

She gave him a motherly glance. "Immediately."

Bill rubbed his hands together, this time gleefully. "I can't tell you how sorry I am, Katie, to cut short our evening. I was having such a wonderful time. I promise you, tomorrow I'll feel one hundred percent better. We'll go swimming."

"We'll do nothing of the sort. Until you're completely better, you're on a chicken-soup-and-hot-tea diet."

"It could be a touch of malaria," he said slowly, drawing a gasp from Katie. "It acts this way. The symptoms came on so suddenly. I haven't had an attack in over a year."

"Malaria!" she cried, astounded at his news. "You have malaria?"

He nodded, then tried to encourage her not to worry. "A touch. It can't hurt you or our son. Do you know anything about malaria?"

"Not a thing."

That pleased him enormously, since his plan wouldn't work if she knew the symptoms of the disease.

"Bill," she went on, "this is no time to think of me or our daughter. You're the important one now. How did you get malaria?"

"On a trip in the jungle. It'll pass."

"You'll need medicine, won't you?"

"I keep quinine pills in my bathrooom bag."

"You poor darling," she cooed. Wrapping her arm about his waist, she propelled him into the hotel. Bill shuddered. In the elevator, people moved away from him. When they reached their rooms, his hand shook so badly, she grabbed the key.

"What can I do?" she asked, growing more concerned. "How can I help?"

He eased away, saying, "I'll take my pills."

"Yes, do that. Then get right into bed. Call me if you need anything. I'll leave the door to our rooms unlocked. Bill, I still think I should call a doctor."

Behind her back, he smiled broadly. "I've had these attacks before. I know what to do. Katie, you're so understanding. I hate to be trouble."

He shed his coat and jacket. Leaving Katie to hang up her coat, he dashed into the bathroom. After rolling up his sleeves, yanking off his tie, and unbuttoning his shirt, he doused his face in ice cold water. He grabbed a face cloth and dripped water on his chest, his neck, his arms. He was shuddering for real when he reentered his room.

He glanced through the open connecting door. Katie's dress was off, giving him a wonderful view of her long legs and enticing black garter belt. How he loved garter belts! He congratulated himself on his Yankee ingenuity.

"Katie," he moaned. "Katie, would you come here a minute please?"

She flew to him. He shivered badly, and she touched his forehead. "You're freezing. I'm phoning the hotel doctor."

He caught her wrist. "No, don't," he begged. "We both know the doctor won't do anything but send me to my own physician. I already took my medicine. Give it time to work."

She nodded, then had a thought. "Would a hot shower help?"

"Good idea," he said, grateful she didn't know a hot shower would be the last thing a sufferer of malaria would need.

"I'll order room service," she said, "and have them send up hot tea."

"I hate tea." He wouldn't mind a bottle of champagne, but that would be stretching his luck.

Katie couldn't argue with a sick man. "What would you like?"

"Nothing, sweetheart. I'll call you if I need you."

In the bathroom, Bill stripped. He turned the cold water on fully, eyed the shower with distaste, and mumbled, "The things I do." He stepped into the shower stall. By the time he stepped out, he froze in earnest. Hopping on one foot, he scooped up the ice bucket, which the maid had filled as he'd requested. Dashing back into the bedroom, he hid the bucket under the bed.

"Katie," he called, interrupting her in the process of taking her nightgown out of her bag. She ran into his room, then stared at him.

"Bill, where are your pajamas?" He had a towel in front of him. Other than that meager protection, he was fully, gloriously naked. Tall, lean, and shivering. Bill's shivering—his practically blue body—convinced her to help first, ask questions later.

Bill's main worry was that he'd heat up too fast. Katie, in a bra, bikini panties, and a black garter belt and stockings, tormented his libido.

"I don't own pajamas," he confessed. "Katie, I'm sorry. I really am." He dove between the sheets as much to hide as to keep his act going. She ran for her robe. He called her back. "Katie, was that baby oil I saw on your dresser earlier?"

"Yes."

He pulled the sheet over his head. "I'm thinking of us, of tomorrow. If we take care of my problem now, it will pass. I'm willing to try anything. Are you?"

She poked her head in the room. "Anything," she said solicitously. "What can I do for you?"

"Would you rub my back? I'm sure it will get my circulation going?"

"Are you sure?"

He peeked above the sheet. "Katie darling." He seesawed his legs, raising and lowering his knees. He beat his arms, giving a good imitation of a man in the throes of an attack.

"Please," he pleaded. "Don't be afraid to touch me. It's not catching. I need you."

He turned over, letting one long arm hang over the side of the bed. He reached for the bucket of ice and palmed several cubes. "Please," he whimpered, muffling his face in the mattress.

Katie leapt into action. Forgetting her robe, she

flew into her room, returning moments later with the oil and a hand towel. She folded the sheet down to expose his back and vigorously bent to the task.

"How does that feel?" she asked, sliding her oiled fingers up and down his back.

"Magic," he said weakly. "You've got magic fingers. Don't stop, Katie."

"I won't, darling."

"Could you go a little lower? It's for a good cause."

She went lower.

The ice cubes had melted in his hand. After drying his hand on the carpet, he reached backward, touching her leg. She jumped. "What's the matter?" he asked.

"Your hand is freezing. Bill, I'd better call the doctor. This isn't working. I wish I knew how to treat someone with malaria. Parts of your body are fevered, the rest freezing."

"I hate doctors. Trust me. You're doing the right thing. I'll turn over. You can do my stomach. Katie, I'd never ask this of you if it weren't absolutely necessary."

Her heart tripped. She hadn't expected to touch Bill so intimately. Immediately she quelled her erotic thoughts and helped him onto his back. When she began to stroke his long torso, he closed his eyes. So did she.

"How does this feel?" she murmured.

"Wonderful, Katie. I'm worried about you, though. Are your hands getting tired?"

"It doesn't matter."

"But it does," he insisted. "Katie, I know of a better way to warm me."

"A hot water bottle," she said, feeling panicky. "I'll phone for several."

"No, don't. They get cold too fast."

She gazed down at him, at his manly chest, at his dear face, his quivering lips. "What can I do?"

He reached up and squeezed her arm. "Body heat works."

"Body heat?" she croaked.

"Mmmm, yes. At home," he lied, "I use a thermal sheet. It helps. Damn, I wish I had brought mine along, but who figured?"

"Bill, darling, are you asking me to warm you with my body?"

He put his hand over his eyes, shivering so violently she nearly tumbled off him. "I'd do it for you, Katie. You know it. Remember the frog, Katie."

She sat back. They were both a lot older than when Bill officiated at her frog's funeral. Still, it wasn't as if he could do anything in his condition. She felt guilty for having kept him outside so long in the cold night air.

Resolutely she capped the bottle of oil, then wiped her hands on the towel. "I'll be right back."

"Oh, thank you," he moaned. "I'll use the bathroom while you're gone."

As soon as she was gone, Bill scrambled out of bed. Katie's hands had set him on fire—a fire he didn't want burning brightly. Not yet. He doused cold water on his face, his arms, his stomach, and his legs. He stood in front of the open window, letting the night air dry his body, yet keep him cold. He hopped back into bed seconds before Katie returned, carrying a bath sheet.

He eyed it warily. "What's that for?"

"I want you to have all the heat you can get.
Put this over you."

He was forced to take it. "Katie, hurry up." He
lifted the blanket a crack, grabbed her arm, and
had her beside him in a flash. He flopped around
like a fish, and she drew him into her arms. He
shivered for an entirely different reason.

"Thank you," he murmured, kneeing the towel
off his stomach. His lips were close to her breast.
His foot rubbed up and down her leg. His hand
traveled the length of her thigh.

"Thank goodness you're here," he said. "You
can't know what you're doing to me. For me."

Katie knew she couldn't take it. For one thing,
her legs kept wanting to open. She told herself it
was wrong to take advantage of a sick man. She
also told herself to remember her resolution and
that list of rules that now seemed foolish and for-
gettable. Bill's fingers strayed to her rib cage.
Somehow she moved down, and his hand cupped
her breast. Even she couldn't prevent the nipple
from nubbing.

"Katie," he whispered in her ear, his speech
slurring.

"Yes, Bill."

"If you stay with me, I'm sure I could sleep."

Katie tried repeating the alphabet backward.

Failing after two tries, she tilted her head up
to look at him. Fortune had graced Bill with a
handsome face and a magnificent body. With a
shock she saw he lay across her like a contented
baby. Her body smoked. "I'd better leave."

"Don't," he mumbled. "I hate being cold. You're
so soft. So sweet. So warm. See, you've warmed
me too. Just think. When I'm better, and you give

me permission, we'll make love. We'll be able to enjoy each other for as long and as often as we please. I'll never be cold again."

In moments she heard his deep, even breathing, signaling sleep.

Katie groaned and collapsed back on the pillow.


Hands stroked her bare skin. A warm mouth closed over her lips, whispering words of love, of encouragement. Katie dreamed she was in Bill's arms. She thrust upward, moving her hips in rhythm with his, and surrended to a severe case of lust. In her dream there were no hampering rules. She could do as she pleased. Touch and be touched. Her tongue went searching on an urgent mission. Her hands slithered across his back, reveling in the rippling musculature. She felt him trace a patternless path to her breasts, nipping and teasing her sensitive flesh. But when he trailed incredibly slow kisses along her belly, a shudder rippled through her, and she grew limp and yielding beneath his touch. She groaned.

Her eyes opened.

This was no dream. Worse, Bill's eyes were closed. She had aroused him in his sleep, had taken advantage of a sick man! Mortified, she eased off the bed. Blushing to the roots of her hair, she tiptoed from the room and closed the door behind her. As she turned on the light, she caught her reflection in the dresser mirror. Her hands flew to her face. She looked as if she'd been thoroughly debauched. Propped against her mirror, mocking her, was her list of rules.

"Fat lot of good you did!" she muttered.

\*       \*       \*

Bill lay on his side, cursing. He threw off the covers and pounded into the bathroom like a man condemned. This time he took a cold shower to cool off.


Bill wandered sleepily into Katie's room the next morning. He would prefer to pass off his attempt to trick her as an excuse to get the job done, but one look at her embarrassed face and he was riddled with guilt. She was his childhood friend, his buddy in nostalgia. She was to be the mother of his child.

He found her sitting up in the huge bed, her hands folded primly over the blanket, her hair tumbling about her bare arms. He wondered if she had slept.

"How are you?" she asked.

His gaze dropped to the alluring sight of her breasts above the scooped edge of her gown. "Much better. Fine, in fact."

"I'm glad." Her lower lip trembled.

"What happened last night?" he asked carefully. "Did I do or say anything I shouldn't have?"

She remembered perfectly. She remembered heated kisses. She remembered wanting him badly. She remembered slinking out of his bed and into hers.

"You were a perfect gentleman," she replied.

He wanted to put his arms around her and love her. His feet moved forward, and before he knew what he was doing, he threw off her covers, sat down on the bed, and pulled her into his arms.

She was soft and fragrant and dewy-eyed. She wilted against him.

His eyes darkened; his lips hovered over hers. Then remorse hit him. Old-fashioned, morality-driven remorse prevented him from carrying through his intended farce. He could feel the perspiration gather on his brow, and released her. "Katie, there's something I'd better confess."

She pulled back, her eyes wide and waiting. Bill's confession had to be serious, she thought, to stop him from kissing her.

"I'm convinced," he said, "that I didn't have an attack of malaria last night."

She went very still. Her arms slipped away from his shoulders. "What did you have?"

His desire to hold her and make love to her had never been so strong. He didn't like it, but he had to tell her the truth.

"A case of the hots."

"A case of the what?" she asked, aghast.

"A case of the hots. I'm a man. Your stupid rules drive me crazy: three days of no kissing; three days after we're married no sex. Then you announce that you need to fantasize—"

"You tricked me!" she yelped. "Have you ever had malaria?"

He chuckled. "Not as far as I know."

"You kissed me. You touched me. Your hands were . . . and mine were . . ."

She went numb. She had touched him too.

He shrugged. "I'm not noble."

Her senses returned abruptly, jarring her to speech. "You can say that again."

"Don't we deserve some gratification?" he railed. "We're wasting two perfectly good beds."

She swept his body with a glacial look. "How did you get your body so cold last night?"

He smiled sheepishly. "Ice cubes and cold showers."

She mouthed his words. *Ice cubes and cold showers.* Drawing an indignant breath, she literally threw him off the bed. "I—I felt sorry for you," she stammered. "I oiled your body. I massaged you."

He quickly volunteered his services. "I'll be happy to massage you too. Katie, you said yourself you wanted me to make you feel loved. All I did was move up the schedule. Admit it. You liked it as much as I did."

She glowered at him.

"How did you keep your hands cold?" she demanded.

"That was easy. I hid the ice bucket under the bed. When I needed to, I grabbed an ice cube."

"So that's why your hand froze my leg."

He grinned.

"You scheming, lying, rotten, no-good imposter. I believed you were ill. I felt sorry for you. I should have guessed you'd resort to trickery. You were trying to get me pregnant."

"I was not, dammit." He stormed into his room, returning with a package of condoms. "Katie, come on. You proved you like me. Heck, a few more minutes and we'd have proven a lot more. Don't make a big deal out of this. You can't blame a guy for trying. You were driving me crazy. We're getting married! Doesn't it count for something?"

She was too busy grinding her teeth to answer. Arms crossed over her breasts, she skewered him with a fiery glare. The thought intruded that she'd like nothing better than to give in, but not yet. "Go away. I need time to think."

"Then think about this," he said, his voice taking on an edge of sarcasm. "As long as you stick to this idiotic timetable, I'm going to do my best to wreck it. It's unnatural for two people about to be married to have two bedrooms. It's ludicrous for you to priss orders at me as if I were a little boy. What kind of nonsense is it to tell me you need time to see if you like me, and then tell me we have to wait three days after we're married to have sex? You yourself said you wanted fondling. I fondled you, and now you're angry. High-school kids have more fun than we do. What's wrong with a little recreational sex? We could both use the exercise."

Katie bounced off the bed. She wore a see-through shortie gown that nearly sent his blood pressure through the roof. "Exercise!" she exclaimed. "You need exercise?"

"You're damned right I do," he shouted. "First you're naked in the tub—"

She whipped around. "Who wears clothes in the bathtub?"

"Don't change the subject Katie, you're a hot little number. Don't waste time denying it. And, yes, we could both use the exercise."

"You're absolutely right," she said, her voice abruptly calm. "I'm going to grant you your wish."

"You are?"

She let him stew a few seconds. "After we're married. Just the way we planned."

A bleak expression quashed his happy smile. He cursed. "Just the way *you* planned, you mean. What am I supposed to do in the meantime?"

She spun past him into his room, sailed back in, and shoved the ice bucket into his chest.

"Here's the perfect solution. Ice cubes and cold showers!"

"Aw hell, Katie." He slumped into a chair, thrusting his long legs out in front of him. "Why be obstinate? You want me as much as I want you. Katie, we came that close."

"Bill, are you in love with me?"

"I don't know how I feel," he admitted.

She drew in a deep breath, and her small, pointed breasts rose accusingly. "We'll keep our arrangement strictly business. Right now I'm going to dress. Then I'm going to eat breakfast. Afterward I'm going for a walk. And then I'm going swimming. You do as you please. If you care to go home, I'll take a bus back."

"No," he said, charging off the chair. "You're not getting rid of me so easily. We are going to enjoy ourselves today if it kills us."

She shook off his hand. "Suit yourself."

Dammit, he thought, returning to his room. He hadn't meant to hurt her feelings. He hadn't expected her to get him so aroused that he felt like a walking tinderbox. Her taste still lingered on his tongue. For a grown man who usually acted honorably, he hadn't been able to resist temptation.

In his gut he suspected where Katie was concerned, he never would.

# Eight

Katie's good humor returned when she was in the tub bathing beneath a billowing cloud of bubbles. A leisurely bath did far more than cleanse her body. It allowed her time to think. After she calmed down and thought about Bill taking ice cold showers, shivering into a mass of goose bumps, and going so far as to hiding a bucket of ice under the bed, she began to see the entire episode as funny. The more she thought of his sneaky actions, the wackier they seemed. Someday she'd enjoy recounting the story to their grandchildren.

She wanted Bill to love her for herself, the way she loved him. Changing his attitude toward marriage took time. Buying time was the reason she'd made up her unorthodox rules of behavior. Bill wasn't wrong when he said they both needed a release. Last night proved it. It had been scary and wonderful and exciting. If she weakened now and made love with him, she'd only be hastening the end, not the beginning, of a long-lasting relationship. The scales weren't tipped in her favor yet. Bill preferred the life of a single person, with the goal of single parenthood. Her goal remained wedded bliss.

Katie completed her less than thrilling summary. Her face flushed from steam, she rose from the tub and studied herself critically in the mirror. She saw an oval face framed by a mass of red hair, confused apple-green eyes, a full mouth, and a slim, short-waisted figure with long legs. Her breasts were small, her hips slightly rounded. As a child she'd tried every remedy she could find to get rid of the hated freckles on her face. Miraculously, they had faded as she grew older. Now only a little path spackled across the bridge of her nose.

She toweled dried and powdered herself, then pulled on a pair of stone-washed jeans, a sea-green blouse, and an embroidered bolero vest. For walking on the boardwalk, she selected the comfort of sneakers. Throwing a heavy jacket over her arm, she crossed the room and knocked on the connecting door.

"Door's open," Bill called as he cupped his hand over the phone. She came inside and laid her jacket down on a chair. To him, Katie looked utterly fetching in her colorful outfit.

An awkward pause filled the air after he concluded his phone call. Their eyes met and memories rivered through them. At the same time their gazes skidded to the bed and sluiced away. Memories of being wrapped in each other's arms, almost becoming one, heated their bodies.

Katie looked back at Bill. His eyes were dark and questioning. "Truce?" he asked.

"Truce," she said, swallowing hard.

He relaxed. "Good, I'm starved. I wouldn't have let either one of us out of this room until we settled this. That was Sy on the phone. There's a problem on one of our jobs, and he's needed there for a few more days. Is it okay with you if I stay at your place right away?"

Katie thought fast. It would have been silly to say no, especially after they had almost been intimate. "Of course. I know how difficult it is to run your business from a hotel room."

Bill breathed a sigh of relief. He hadn't known how she would take his request. "After Sy arrives, I'll go over the names of people in Cape May who do restoration work. Sy's been with the company longer than I have. He and my uncle John started together. Sy never wanted to be in management, though. He says his pleasure is in doing the work, feeling the wood. He's the best foreman in the business. And he's a real character. He says what's on his mind, but what he doesn't know about restoration isn't worth knowing. Also, we'll use local talent for everything but the intricate detailed work."

She walked over to him, standing close enough for him to smell her floral perfume. For a moment he absorbed her scent, lighter now than when she lay in his arms. With effort, he recalled what he'd been saying.

"We'll repair and paint the outside right away. You'll need to look at tile and counter samples. Katie . . ." He reached out to take her hand. "I may have to fly to Arizona to meet with one of my clients this week."

An alarm bell sounded. "Bill, perhaps we ought to wait."

"Don't be silly. The ground hasn't frozen yet. The men can work outside. The quicker the house is in shape, the quicker we'll get married."

And the quicker he'll become a single father, she thought.

The December day set a record of seventy-three degrees, resulting in throngs of people wandering the boardwalk. Much had changed since Bill had last visited the gambling mecca of the East Coast. Besides numerous new hotels and casinos, there were new businesses.

"The weather is glorious," Katie said as she stripped off her jacket. "But then again, living in California, you're probably not as impressed as I am."

Behind them a whistle tooted. They stepped aside for the jitney to pass. It traveled from one end of the boardwalk to the other, picking up and depositing people along the way.

"Katie, my house isn't near the ocean. It's inland in Orange County in a town called Irvine. We welcome the wind to clear the Los Angeles basin of smog."

A boisterous group of children skidded by on skateboards. "I thought you loved your house."

He squeezed her hand. "I do, but it's only a house, which I'll keep so I have a place to live in when I'm out there. I'll love being here more."

The baby, she thought.

As if he'd read her mind, he said, "There's a story I want to tell you about a wise Indian whose name was Chief Seattle. He preached the importance of the circle. It was his belief that no matter how much a man wanders the earth, he always comes full circle to find his happiness. This he does by passing on his seed to the next generation. Chief Seattle understood the true meaning of immortality."

Bill smiled. "By today's standards, the chief might seem a male chauvinist since he neglected to include women, but I like to think he meant women too. Katie, you and I are part of the same circle."

Bill stood in the shining light, his features heightened by the rays of sun splashing on his face. His words made a deep impression on her. She squeezed his hand and before she could stop herself placed a kiss on his lips. A fleeting thought crossed her mind. Bill intended to break the circle by returning to his single status.

"How about that swim now?" he asked.

"You're on," she said, anxious for the diversion.

The hotel's pool was larger than Olympic size, with several diving boards at different heights above the water. Katie, wearing a two-piece aqua bathing suit, stood poised on the low board, ten meters above the water. Bill watched from the side, admiring her firm figure, the long column of her legs, and her small but full breasts pressing tautly against the fabric. After a few seconds he managed to drag his spellbound gaze away from her body and concentrate on her dive.

"Don't over rotate," he instructed. "Watch your tuck position."

"Quit worrying," she yelled down. Concentrating fully, she checked her preparation for the dive. Diving from the low board required precise platform skills. Doing this dive for Bill, she jumped high and away, executing a one-and-one-half backward somersault. She knifed the water with a straight cut.

Bill slapped his knee and let out a tense breath. Shoulder and back injuries were the main concerns divers faced, and Katie had told him she hadn't dived in years.

She swam to the edge of the pool, whipping the hair from her face, her eyes alight with mischief. She had done well and was pleased.

"Good going, Katie. Nice tuck position. You kept your legs straight. It was a fine, solid dive. Out before you overdo it the first time."

"How about a race?" she challenged.

He grinned. He'd never been able to resist that kind of temptation. "You're on, Red."

He hit the water with a neat running dive, surfacing close to her. He locked his strong legs around her. "Give me a kiss for luck first."

She hooted. "No way. I'm going to win."

His hands grasped her shoulders, trapping her. He studied her fine eyelashes, tipped with tiny, jeweled droplets of water. Her eyes still glistened with the success of her dive. "Then I'll give you a kiss for luck," he said, and did so, in full view of about ten onlookers.

They raced the length of the pool and back. He won. Twice.

"No fair," she grumbled. Her arms ached from being out of shape. Her legs were tired. She was panting. She was also having the time of her life. "Your legs are longer."

"That's not all," he quipped, shamelessly rubbing against her. When she feebly protested, he nipped her ear. "I can kiss you all I want. The three days are up."

"Since when did you pay attention to anything I asked?"

"I never intended to. I just want you to know the three days are over."

Bill's infectious spirits moved into high gear. They stayed in the water for another half hour before he hustled her out. They showered, changed, and returned to the action area of the hotel. Katie lost ten dollars to a one-armed bandit. Bill broke even. They decided it was time to leave the clatter of the casinos, opting for the outdoors.

Strolling hand in hand, they paused to inspect the many antique shops along the boardwalk. For lunch they decided on chili dogs, asking the vendor to pile on the works. They sat on a bench facing the ocean, eating their hot dogs and sharing a large bag of French fries. They washed their food down with cream soda. Lazily content, they tossed bread crumbs to the pigeons.

Eventually they wandered into a noisy arcade and played the pinball machines. Bumping hips and hands, they disputed every game, griping loudly that the other had cheated. Laughing, they came back outside and strolled along the beach, delighted with the unseasonably warm weather. Tiring of that, Katie dragged Bill inside a two-story mall shaped like a ship. She quickly located a sweet shop and scouted it out.

"Smart merchandising," she said when they were back outside and settled on a bench. "The more I think about it, Bill, the more I'm convinced I should branch out into the mail-order business. It's right. I can feel it. Phyllis agrees. I'm going to take the plunge and do it."

"Good for you," Bill said, though he was less interested in her business than he was in her luminous skin, her elegant profile, her hair like red-gold fire in the sun. Her attention had been caught by a seagull soaring close to the water's edge. She turned to him and smiled, a promising smile that had him catching his breath.

"Katie, how would you like me to build you a swimming pool with a retractable roof? It can be an addition to the house."

Whenever he talked of her house she felt increasingly uncomfortable, as if it and she were down payments on his future. If she could, she'd postpone the work indefinitely. The thought prompted her answer. "It's too much of an extravagance."

"Not really," he argued. "We'd both use it."

Her stomach lurched, her good mood soured by the knowledge that his desire for her was temporary, while hers was permanent. He wanted her for the baby, not for what they would mean to each other.

"Katie, think of our son," he said, unwittingly confirming her theory. "We both want him to swim."

"Her," she corrected him automatically.

"We'll never know until we try, will we?" he asked. "Katie, I want you to set a marriage date."

The thought of setting a date was like a prickly thorn in her side. She looked at him. He was sleekly handsome with intelligent eyes, a square, cleft chin, and a straight nose. He'd make a fabulous groom—and a lousy temporary husband!

Their eyes met. "I was thinking soon," he added, his voice an intimate whisper.

She caught her breath. He sent her heart aflutter. "But our plans . . . ?"

"Let's elope."

Katie fought down panic. She wanted romance. Above all she wanted the natural order of things. It wasn't that she required a large wedding. She would have preferred walking down the aisle, her father giving her away. She would have liked her mother to see her in a bridal gown and Phyllis to be her matron of honor. She would have liked Charlie to be the ring bearer. But under the circumstances, she wouldn't want any of that. It would ring false.

She managed to keep her expression bland, yet her true feelings were dangerously close to the surface. "Bill, you're getting ahead of yourself again."

He chuckled, and his fingers gently grazed her cheek. His gaze dropped to her lips, to her breasts.

"Katie," he said wryly, staring into her eyes, "I'm so far behind myself it isn't funny."

She knew the look well, the competitive spirit that overcame him when goals were just beyond his reach. She knew how his body coiled, how his stance changed when he set out to win.

Katie was getting cold feet. Bill knew it. He'd been pushing her too hard, asking her for decisions she wasn't ready to make. Katie wasn't the girl he remembered, not that he was complaining.

His fascination with her continually surprised him.

"How many of your friends have children?" she suddenly asked.

He rested his hand on his updrawn knee. "Most do. Most are divorced too."

"Is that why you want your freedom?"

He ran both hands through his hair, then clasped them behind his head. For seconds he stared at the ocean. It occurred to him that this was a mighty odd conversation, but Katie deserved an honest answer.

"I had a friend named Gil Pleasant. We met shortly after I graduated from college. Gil is a big blond Swede who had a driving ambition to become a famous architect. I was already working for my uncle, so I asked Uncle John to hire Gil. During the summer, Gil and I met a girl named Nancy. We were restoring her father's house. Gil fell for Nancy in a big way. They married four months later. Within a year Nancy became pregnant. Gil was the proudest dad you ever saw. Those two had what I called the perfect marriage.

"Nancy's father introduced Gil to the head of a major architectural firm, specializing in office complexes throughout the Southwest. Gil was hired and had to travel. Not that much, but when he did he took pictures of Nancy and his son to show everyone.

"Nancy." Bill shook his head. "Nancy had straight jet-black hair that fell to her tush. A tush she wiggled effectively, I might add. I personally knew a dozen men who wanted her."

"Did you?" Katie asked.

"No. She reminded me of Janice."

"I thought you liked Janice."

"Janice is what men call an easy lay. She's all things to all men."

Katie's heart thrummed at the news. Bill fell silent.

She reached out tentatively, urging him to continue. "Go on, please."

He shrugged. "That's it. Nancy got bored. She cheated on Gil. One day she announced she wanted a divorce. Gil fell apart. Totally snapped. He'd missed the warning signs. The poor dope thought he had it all. Anyway, when Nancy started her divorce action, Gil stopped working for the firm. He started drinking heavily. The last I heard, he was doing odd jobs."

She stared at him, amazed. "Are you saying their divorce soured you on marriage?"

"No." He eyed her dubiously. "I'm not that stupid."

"Then what?" she asked. Pressure built within her as she waited to learn the reason for Bill's attitude toward marriage.

He studied the backs of his hands. "I'm saying that Gil let himself in for a fall. I like my life the way it is, except for wanting a child, so why rock the boat?"

Katie wanted to shake some sense into him. "Were he and Nancy friends?"

He cocked his head to one side and looked at her. "They married. I'd say that's pretty friendly, wouldn't you?"

"They could have been lovers and not friends."

An expression of wariness slipped over his face. "Meaning?"

"Meaning," she replied, straining to hold her

patience in check, "it's better to be both. Like your parents, for instance."

Or like us, she added silently, if you'd give us a chance.

He snapped his head up sharply. His jaw tensed, hardening with obstinacy. "Let's change the subject."

She wouldn't. If she hadn't known him so well, she might have been put off by his look. Her new-found knowledge of Bill affected her more than his sad story. It inexplicably strengthened her will to prove that marriage could be a cherished part-nership based on mutual love and respect. She realized now why he was marriage shy. He was scared. He wasn't the great hero she had made him out to be, nor the villain in the piece for wanting his freedom. He was a vulnerable, sensi-tive man. Also a nut. A nut she was determined to crack!

"Whether you admit it or not," she said, "your friend Gil had other choices. We all do." It was on the tip of her tongue to tell him he was frightened of marriage thanks to his friends' failures. Instead, she decided to change tactics.

He was silhouetted against the sun, his profile classic and beautiful. She knew that when he asked her again to make love to him, sticking to her resolve would be harder than ever. She tallied up his manly attributes: his square jaw signaling determination, his rugged countenance, the com-pelling hint of danger in his stance, the arresting manner in which he looked at her, the humor she knew lurked just beneath the surface.

"Bill," she began, picking her way carefully, "I'm beginning to see your point. I, too, know people who have divorced. It can be a messy process. So what you're saying is that marriage is passé."

"You agree with me?" he asked suspiciously. "Since when?"

"Gradually, I admit. I think I've been afraid to give in to my preconceived notions. In a way, playing the devil's advocate has given me a chance to test my outdated theories. I'm a creature of habit, I suppose. Don't forget I was raised to believe in certain traditions. I can't deny that it took a while to change, but your recounting of Gil and Nancy's divorce story clinched it. You're absolutely right. Why let ourselves be miserable? It stands to reason that if most of your friends are divorced, it's inevitable we will be too. Why put ourselves through rounds of arguments? The more I think about it, the better I like the whole idea. We both agree we want a child. I'm sure I can fantasize my way through it. There's no reason not to think so. Last night proved I'm capable of fantasizing anything—"

"See here!" Bill interrupted. Frowning, he pounded a fist against his knee. "That wasn't just anything, Katie. That's a pretty broad generalization for what went on between us."

She shushed him. "I won't quibble. Call it what you want. My point is, I'm advising you to buy the house next door. We'll be one of the very few amicably divorced couples. I'm grateful we've had this discussion."

She patted his arm. "Don't you feel one hundred percent better? I do. You've given me a whole new lease on life. It's as if I have permission to do whatever I please, whenever I please. Lots of people do, I know, but for me it's a revelation."

Anything resembling cheerfulness fled from Bill's face. "You're a lot different from the way I remembered you."

She smiled brilliantly. "Why thank you. That's one of the nicest compliments you could have paid me. Tonight we'll write out the divorce agreement. As long as we're so amicable, we can avoid attorneys' fees. Why involve a bunch of lawyers who'll muck it up with legalese? Go ahead and build the pool. We'll all use it."

Bill glowered. "Who's all?"

Smiling serenely, she counted on her fingers, "You, me, our daughter, my boyfriends, or lovers—"

He exploded off the bench. A shaft of dread sliced through him. He strode to the edge of the boardwalk, then stomped back to her. "Like hell!" In an ominous tone, he blurted out what he'd been thinking for days. "I'll be damned if I'm going to baby-sit while my wife dates other men."

Katie breathed a sigh of relief.

# Nine

Bill leaned against the door frame, watching Katie spray perfume on her wrists and her neck. "Where's the rest of your dress? Isn't there a stole to go with it? You'll get cold."

Delighting in his grouchy complaint, she raised her arms and twirled around. Her new, racy, blue sequined dress covered her from the top of her breasts to about mid-thigh, and lovingly conformed to everything in between.

"What you see is what you get," she quipped.

"I'm going to have to fight the men away," he muttered.

Turning to the mirror, she checked her makeup, attached her earrings, and handed Bill her necklace. "Fasten the catch for me, please." She angled her head, holding her long hair to the side.

"Are you trying to make me jealous?" he asked, running his fingers lightly along the column of her neck.

She got control of herself and said, "Don't be ridiculous. Why would I do that?" She gazed up at him in the mirror. "Bill, be practical. Have I ever done anything to make you jealous? Why should I? We're friends. Friends treat each other with consideration. Speaking of consideration, there's writing paper in the desk. Jot down whatever you think is fair. You can have visitation rights whenever you want."

"You're awfully eager for this divorce, aren't you?"

She smiled, cheerful in the face of his obvious irritation. "Not awfully. I'm practical." She extended her leg, smoothing her stocking. "You yourself said it's good business to know beforehand where we stand." Turning her back, she stepped into her pumps. "Tonight's our last night. What shall we do?"

"For starters? This. This is what I want to do."

He settled his mouth on hers for a long, involved kiss. His silky tongue stroked and lavished the sweet recess of her mouth. He sucked gently on her lips, then applied pressure. He teased, he tormented, he took.

Katie returned his kiss with equal ardor. She wrapped her arms about his neck, pressing her belly against his. Through his clothing, she felt his rigid reaction. She nuzzled his neck for good measure, taking the lead. Her fingers slid into the soft hair at his nape, her body arching to his. A shudder shook his powerful frame. Gently she eased away, tormented by the pleasure-pain, the sense of wonderment he evoked deep within her soul.

Unwilling to relinquish her, he pulled her possessively back, holding her tight against him, feeling the elegant length of his bride-to-be. He nibbled the base of her throat and felt her pulse race beneath his lips. He wanted her, wanted to place her on the bed behind them and kiss the satiny smooth valley between her breasts. He didn't feel it necessary to match the slow pace she seemed only too delighted to follow.

They caressed and stroked and clung, then felt a sense of loss as they drew away by slow degrees, thighs, hips, breasts.

"Divorcing you is going to be a cinch," she said, lying through her teeth. "Look how friendly we are."

"Katie," he growled. "Marrying me is going to be a hell of a lot more friendly."

"I'm hungry," she said evasively. "We'd better go."

He cupped her neck with his hand. "Who wants to eat when we can make out?"

She smiled radiantly. "I do."

He looked at the bed, then at her. He thought he would drown in the shimmering greenness of her eyes. "What a waste."

Still, they had fun that evening. From long-standing habit, Bill and Katie were used to enjoying each other's company. At the restaurant he tucked her securely beneath his arm as they walked to the table for two.

"None of this assembly line eating for us tonight. I want you for myself." He smiled at her with tenderness. "Katie, you look ravishing."

"So do you," she said, meaning it. In a dark blue suit, white shirt, and blue tie, he was receiving more than a few glances of admiration from the other women.

The tone of the evening differed from that of the night before, for between them lay the knowledge they'd shared a bed, even for a short time. Every accidental or casual touch, every evocative glance, stirred sensual memories. Although her willpower was shaky, Katie hung on to her resolve—until she made the mistake of agreeing to learn to dance the Lambada, the hot Brazilian dance craze sweeping the night spots. In high-spirited fun, they gyrated to the sexy beat of the music. Yet as every part of them touched—pelvis to pelvis, thigh to thigh, chest to chest—teasing, undulating, igniting, the fun was seared away by hot desire. By the end of the dance they were so hungry for each other, she could no more deny him than she could stop the sun from rising.

His eyes were dark burning pools. "Katie?"

Rules that were impossible to keep were meant to be broken, she realized. She slipped her hand in his.

Katie floated in space. She was in Bill's bed, lying naked on cool satin sheets, surrounded by a gossamer silk tent. Vanilla-scented incense perfumed the air. She filled her lungs with a more heady perfume—Bill. Her flesh tingled as his hand whispered across her. She tried to lie perfectly still, savoring each touch, each exploration. She felt him kiss her breasts, first one, then the other. Her nipples rose. She moaned.

Her hands slid up his back, bringing his mouth back to the breasts he'd abandoned as his lips made exquisite love to the rest of her body. She held him for what seemed forever, driving her fingers into his hair. She thought of the wondrous urgency in his touch, and then she stopped thinking. Her heart pounded as he continued to fondle her, arouse her to a fevered pitch.

Her flesh came alive under his touch. Murmuring praise, lips moved softly against lips. Wild blood coursed through her veins. Katie had said she wanted to be loved. He was all she could ever want or hope to want. Her passion and excitement communicated to him.

She touched him, held him, caressed him, sated herself with him. Positions changed. Passions increased. She kissed him as he had kissed her. Her lips journeyed boldly from mouth to chest and lower. Bill moaned. He took her hand away, brought her face-to-face in the darkness. "Katie, my precious sweet Katie." For a brief moment they separated, and she knew there would be no baby made that night.

He reached for her again, crushing her with a fierce kiss. Her breasts were flattened against his chest, her curves a perfect fit to the muscular planes of his body. Aggressively, he claimed her mouth. Tenderly, he parted her thighs. His fingers touched that most secret place of all, driving her senses into delicious tremors. The sounds of her passion inflamed him, setting him afire with need.

Katie's heart swelled with love. Her eyes glazed with desire. She gave herself to him uninhibitedly, trusting him with her heart, her soul, her body. When he placed himself between her legs, she opened for him as naturally as though the act were preordained. She guided him with her fingers, stroking him with her hand, urging him deeper and deeper into her hot, passion-filled body.

Bill watched her lovely face as he entered her, heard the tiny gasps of her breathing. He took delight in her pleasure, finding his satisfaction in hers. Their bodies melded, strained with sweet friction, thrust with ragged desire, erupted with victorious completion. And when it was over, he buried his face in the hollow of her neck. A sense of well-being, of completeness, filled him, and the unfamiliarity of it gave rise to his announcement.

"Katie, we'll be married immediately."

Katie lay still. She heard the sounds of the world coming back into her consciousness. Candles sputtered. Sheets rustled. An elevator door opened and people spoke beyond their door, their voices fading as they passed. The scent of sex swirled over the bed.

She couldn't trust herself to speak. She'd made violent, tender, exquisite, perfect love with Bill. Not once had he said he loved her. He'd told her she was beautiful. He wanted to marry her right away. Without mutual love, marriage meant nothing. A tear slid down her cheek. She turned on her side, away from him.

"No, Bill. Let's not rush things."

Bill slipped from the bed and stumbled into the bathroom. He returned with a towel slung low on his hips. His face dripped with water as if he'd hurriedly washed it. He handed her a washcloth and towel. Katie pulled the sheet up to her chin.

"Isn't that a bit like closing the barn door once the horse is out?" he asked, "Why won't you marry me right away? We've already proved we can't live by your silly rules. Nor should we."

"You want to start trying for the baby right away?" she asked.

His heated look answered her, but he confirmed it, asking, "What do you think?"

"I need time, Bill."

He stared at her for a long moment. "Time? We've known each other over twenty-five years. Isn't that long enough? Katie, what we had wasn't just good sex or recreational sex. It was terrific sex. You were terrific. We were terrific."

He sat down on the bed and drew her to him. "Tell me what's wrong. Tell me and I'll make it right."

She pulled away from him. How could she tell him all he needed was to say one little word? Katie was shattered. When she should have been deliriously happy, she wanted to sob her heart out. Slowly, she disentangled herself from him and went in search of her clothes.

"Bill, I'll marry you, but I'd prefer sticking to our original plans. Please, don't ask more of me."

"Katie," he said, confused and more than a little hurt. "Why do you sound as if marrying me is a death sentence?"

In a curious way, Katie realized, his choice of words sounded prophetic. The sooner she married him, the sooner she'd lose him.

The next morning, Katie's hot bath failed to soothe her. She vacillated between being sorry and glad she'd made love with Bill. She'd fallen willingly into his bed, regardless of all her petty schemes. Bill was Bill, a charming, strong-minded man. He wasn't about to change. Did she have the right to change him, even if it were possible? So where did giving herself to him leave her?

It left her frustrated and miserable and aching for him. Having known his intimate caress, she loved him more than ever. She felt utterly defenseless. Perhaps she ought to forget her dream and settle for what Bill offered. Yet if she did, she wouldn't be true to herself. Katie discarded the idea.

Bill showered, shaved, nicked himself twice, stuck bits of tissue on the cuts, then dressed, not realizing his socks didn't match.

"Women!" He spat it like a curse word as he paced the room, absently massaging the back of his neck. Katie had hied herself off to the tub again. He was coming to hate the sound of water. He was sorely tempted to barge in on her and demand that she give him one good reason why they shouldn't marry immediately, especially since they were now lovers. He simply couldn't figure her reaction. They had been friends all their lives. They had fun together. They could speak on any subject—except whatever it was that bothered her now. He didn't even want to let himself think about the lovemaking they'd shared. If he did, he'd whip into the bathroom, drag Katie out of the tub, and do it all over again.

Her body was perfect: small, sexy, seductive. Her skin was smooth and fragrant. That she had responded to him was a fact. He doubted she'd known the depths of her own passion. She was as lusty a lover as he. So why her refusal? Unless she didn't really want to marry him and have his child.

The thought that she might not want him chilled him more than the idea of not having a son with her. He'd come home knowing exactly what he wanted from life, how he wanted to get it. What he hadn't figured on was his response to Katie. The more he was with her, the more he wanted her. What was happening to him?

Before he left the room, he paused for one last look in the mirror and saw the bits of paper he'd struck on his chin. He tore the small pieces of tissue off, and the cuts started bleeding again.

"Figures," he mumbled. He couldn't remember the last time he'd cut himself shaving. Then again he couldn't remember wanting a woman as much as he wanted Katie.

Filled with misgivings and self-doubt, Bill checked them out of the hotel. As he stowed their bags in the car, he vowed to say nothing to upset her. During the drive home, Katie talked about Sweet Mischief and expanded her ideas from the mail-order business to developing a new advertising campaign. He saw the sense to it and told her so, although he had to force himself to concentrate. A few minutes later he saw a diner.

"Let's eat," he said, swinging into the parking lot.

The waitress led them to a booth. They busied themselves behind their menus. Their bacon and eggs arrived, and they dived into the meal as a defense against talking. He ate mechanically, she absentmindedly. He folded his napkin, she shredded hers. He slammed his empty cup on the saucer, hers rattled.

"Katie, we'd better talk about this."

"If you're worried about my keeping my part of the bargain, don't. If you're questioning your manliness, don't. You're an excellent lover."

He cringed, then let his anger show. "I'm also an excellent driver, an excellent bridge player, an excellent swimmer. I'm excellent in my work, excellent to the people who work for me. I'm so excellent, it's disgusting."

"I didn't mean to insult you."

"I wish you'd tell me what you do mean." He leaned toward her and lowered his voice. "I'm sitting here thinking about you naked in my arms with your legs wrapped around my waist and me inside you. I wanted to make love to you again last night. Instead you swept off the bed, acting as though we'd made a mistake. Lady, you're a hard one to figure."

She blushed. Despite his heated recital, she felt lonely and teary. Sex without love was simply a physical release. She didn't want to tell him how she felt and risk losing him. He needed to discover certain truths on his own.

"I told you I needed time."

He signaled for the check. "Take all the time you need." He slapped down the money and slid off the booth, heading for the car.


Bill moved his belongings into her house, then went to pick up Samson at Sally and Eric Knudsen's. Eric gave him a message for Katie: the new carpeting was in and looked fine. He was sure Katie would approve.

Samson purred like a locomotive when he saw Katie. "I'm going to get started on a few minor jobs," Bill said, leaving her to play with the kitten.

The kitten scampered up the stairs into her bedroom, jumped onto the bed, and curled up into a ball. Katie quickly unpacked, then changed into work clothes, tying a bandana over her head. If Bill was going to work, she might as well work too. Keeping busy was better than fighting.

She marched into the dining room and was moving the heavy table aside when Bill appeared in the doorway. He had on a blue cambric shirt and jeans.

"What do you think you're doing?" he demanded.

"I'm going to wash the chandelier. I can't very well do that without standing on a ladder, can I?"

"This room's going to be painted. Why can't it wait?"

"I'll cover it," she said. "I feel like washing the chandelier."

"Get out of the way. I'll move the damn table." He did. "Where's the ladder?"

"In the garage."

He came back with it and set it up. "Next time, ask. You're too little to carry that thing."

"I've been dragging this ladder around for years."

"Not any more." He was gone before she could reply.

Katie mixed vinegar and water in a bucket, tucked several rags under her arm, and climbed the ladder. She didn't care whether it made sense to wash the chandelier or not. She knew why Bill was angry. Tough!

A few minutes later he called. "Katie, come up here a minute."

She slapped the rag into the bucket, spewing water over the side. "Now? I'm busy. Can't it wait?"

"No."

She removed her rubber gloves and climbed down the ladder. She ran up the stairs only to find Bill adjusting a new handle on her bedroom door. He'd gotten her all the way up there to look at a door handle! Considering the charged emotions between them since their return from Atlantic City, she vowed to remain outwardly unruffled.

"Hand me that screwdriver," he said. He gave the screw a final turn. "There that's better. What do you think?"

She put her hands on her hips, dipped her head, stepped forward, then backward. "I liked it when I picked it out. I've got my hands full washing the crystals on the chandelier. Couldn't this have waited?"

He snatched up his toolbox, crossed to the window seat at the end of the hall, and peered out the window. "I don't like the idea of Sy alone here with you. I've decided to postpone my trip to Arizona until he leaves."

"He isn't here yet. Besides, I thought you said he's a nice man."

Bill's brow furrowed. "Never mind what I said."

Her eyebrows went up like two question marks. "You mean he isn't nice?"

"Are you trying to make me angry?"

She could have told him he was already. "No." She sighed. "Please explain yourself."

"I've changed my mind. That's all there is to it. It's not proper."

"Not proper?" She shook her head. "Your own words. 'Sy's as harmless as a pussy cat.' You said all he talks about is his wife and children."

They exchanged a long, telling glance before Bill countered, "No man's harmless."

"Does that include you?"

His mouth tightened and his jaw tensed. "Leave it alone, Katie. I'm not in the mood. That's all I wanted to say."

She stomped past him. "Yes, your highness!"

The next time he interrupted her, he insisted that she check samples of paint chips. Down she came from the ladder. Up the stairs she climbed. "This!" She pointed, matching his churlish behavior. "This color and this color! Satisfied?"

"You chose white."

She gave up all pretense at civility. "Sue me. I like white. Anyway it's eggshell, buff, and off-white, for your information!"

He wouldn't give her the satisfaction. "Don't you dare choose white for the outside." White was the one color most shied away from. At the turn of the century it was considered bad taste.

A short while later he yelled down that he was hungry.

She squared off and yelled back, "Fix yourself a sandwich! You know where the refrigerator is."

He was in the dining room in a flash, his hands bracing the ladder. "I'll fix two. Get down from there and take a break."

"I don't need one!"

"I don't like eating alone!"

They ate with the kitten dancing between them.

They no sooner had finished when he said, "I want you to look at the wallpaper samples."

She scarcely managed to keep from throwing her plate at him. "What about the chandelier?"

"Do it later."

It went on like that all day. They walked the fine line between testiness and arguing and ended up arguing about everything. By the time Katie said good night, she was ready to strangle him.

She lay in her bed fuming, staying there out of perversity. Her great plan seemed doomed to failure. There she was, alone, while he was downstairs watching television. In time her anger subsided, leaving her empty and miserable. After a while she heard him come upstairs and go into the bathroom. Then she remembered she'd forgotten to supply him with toothpaste.

He was shaving when she knocked on the bathroom door. He swabbed a towel across his face, then slung it around his neck. In deference to her and Sy, who would be arriving soon, he'd purchased a pair of pajamas. Wearing nothing but the bottoms, he opened the door to let her in. On the floor, his portable radio was tuned to a soft rock station.

Katie wore the chenille robe she'd had on the night he'd first touched her breast. Knowing what he knew now, the sight brought an instant ache to his loins. Sleeping under the same roof and not being able to share her bed put him in a cranky mood. A grim smile curved his lips, then died away. His hungry gaze flew to her face.

Her hair was piled on top of her head, fighting the clasp to come free. Wisps of hair framed a face that was scrubbed shiny as an apple. Her eyes gleamed behind the glasses she wore instead of her contacts. On her feet were a pair of fuzzy mules. Her toenails were painted red.

Bill waited for her to speak. When she didn't, he did. "You've been in the tub again, haven't you?" He sniffed the air. "I can smell you. You've wearing your flower scent."

"It's my powder," she said awkwardly, looking everywhere but at him.

The room was large, with white and blue tiles on the walls. It had a free-standing clawfoot tub and a shower stall that had been added by her parents. Katie had bought bathroom carpeting, a plush blue, to cover the floor. A high window faced west, capable of snatching the last of the afternoon sun like a miser.

But it wasn't afternoon. It was dark out, with a quarter moon in the sky and two nervous people warily avoiding each other's eyes

Katie's gaze fell on the sink. It was carved from one piece of Carrara marble, and Bill's toilet articles lined the ledge: a can of shaving cream, a Bic razor, aftershave lotion, a stiff-bristled hairbrush, and a yellow toothbrush.

"You don't use an electric razor," she said, as if discovering a momentous bit of information she hadn't learned in Atlantic City.

"No. I gave up on electric shavers. Is there something you want?"

"Yes," she began, then stopped. She rubbed her lips together, pressed a hand to her heart. Digging in her robe pocket, she pulled out a tube of toothpaste and thrust it at him. "I—I heard you in here and remembered I hadn't stocked the medicine cabinet with toothpaste. I hope the brand is okay."

"I brought my own, but this is fine." He took it, his fingers lingering on hers. Against his will, the memory of them together came back so strong, his stomach felt hard as a rock. "Supper was delicious," he said.

"I'm glad." She looked down at her feet, agonizing on what to say next. They behaved more like two strangers than recent lovers. "Is there anything else you need? Magazines? Books? I've got a few mysteries, if you'd like."

He was thinking that under normal circumstances they would have made love at least four times by now.

"Katie, this is nuts," he muttered, moving to her. "I want you. I think you want me too. You've agreed to marry me, yet you treat me as though I were a pariah instead of the man you're going to marry."

"And give back his freedom," she said quietly.

His shoulders sagged; his fists curled and uncurled. She couldn't know that it was the word freedom that had him gnashing his teeth. He guessed she had finally gotten up the gumption to tell him what he suspected.

She wanted to cancel their deal.

He heard himself ask, "Didn't I satisfy you, Katie? We should be able to talk this out. It's important."

An image of them climaxing together sped through her mind. She blushed as red as her hair. Her words choked in her throat.

At length he tipped up her chin, forcing her to look at him. The light fixture glowed over her head, spotlighting her, highlighting her embarrassment. She expelled a shallow breath. He might not be in love with her as she was with him, but she'd hurt him deeply.

"Bill, it was wonderful. Don't think that, please."

He gazed into her eyes, seeing the shyness there and the memory, and a smile curved his lips. He slid his hands over her shoulders, drawing her to him, and buried his face in her neck. "I didn't know what to think, Katie. One minute the two of us are soaring, the next it's the pits. What should I have thought?"

She kissed him, more as an apology than to fan the flames of passion. His fingers found the front of her robe, opening it for his inspection. "You're so beautiful," he said, working the robe off her shoulders and down her arms. It and her nightgown pooled on the floor.

"We can't," she protested.

"Why not? I'm ready to explode." He reached into his toilet bag for protection.

"There are bedrooms," she murmured. "We're in the bathroom for goodness' sake."

"Be adventurous, Katie."

He lowered his head, taking her breast in his mouth, flicking his tongue across the nipple until she moaned. She clasped his head to her. He shifted slightly, letting her feel his raging need. She nuzzled against him. Her fingers slipped between the elastic band of his pajamas and his skin. She closed her hand around him, pleased by the sound he made. Together they dropped to the carpet. He braced himself above her, impatiently hooking her legs around his waist.

"I can't believe we're doing this," she said.

He kissed her jaw, her chin, her eyelids. "It's either this or go blind."

She laughed. "That's nonsense."

His answer was to push himself inside her welcoming heat, shutting off all verbal communication. She wrapped her arms around his neck and clung to him. He teased her with his finger. Her eyes shot open, and he smothered her gasp with his mouth. He moved, stroking in and out, alternating his rhythm.

And then he withdrew from her, only to be brought back down hard. She was kissing him, taking him in her hands, driving him as mad as he'd driven her. Their mouths met in frenzied kisses, tongues invading deep. Their bodies slickened, glistened.

He clenched his jaw, afraid the climax would come too soon. Lifting his head, he cupped her face in his hands. He saw her compelling green eyes, the smattering of freckles across her pert nose, her swollen, kissable lips.

"Ah Katie. Have you any idea what you do to me?"

Tendrils of feeling coiled deep within her. "And you me," she said honestly. Whatever else happened between them, she couldn't deny this rapture.

He took her hand away and filled her again: agile, tense, strong. She clutched his arms, felt his corded muscles strain, and then as his tempo increased, she arched her back. He cried out, taking them both over the edge, shuddering his release in unison with hers.

He lay spent on top of her, weak and strong at once. Both had their eyes closed, their breaths coming in short pants, evening out as the air cooled their sweaty bodies. Her hand lay listlessly on his back; his draped limply on her neck. Gradually he raised his head and dropped a kiss on her lips. When he found the strength, he rolled to the side.

The rock music had changed to a heavy metal beat. The radiator hissed. Katie was conscious of lying on the floor. She let her eyes drift open. Bill lay on his side looking at her.

A rebellious flush flooded her cheeks. She giggled.

"What is it?" he mumbled.

"I was thinking about your knees," she said impudently. "This can't be good for them."

He chuckled and kissed her belly button. "Sweetheart, I wasn't thinking about my knees, or couldn't you tell?"

She lay as he'd left her: on the floor with her arms outstretched, thoroughly debauched. "Right. We did it for your eyesight."

She thought again that he hadn't said he loved her and of her resolve. "The more I sample your free and easy life-style, the more I like it. Do you do this often?"

He grinned. "Only when absolutely necessary."

She braced herself up on her elbow. "I'm going to do it too."

"Do what?" he asked.

"Take my pleasures in unorthodox ways." She sat up. "You know, the longer I'm with you, the more I'm convinced you're right to want our freedom." She rose and put on her robe.

"Don't go." He wanted to take a shower with her.

She smiled and kissed his chin. "Oh, but I have to. It's part of my freedom of choice. I'm going to make out the terms of our divorce." She paused, her hand on the knob, and looked back over her shoulder. "Don't worry, darling. With this arrangement, I might even find time for you."

He scowled. The less he wanted his freedom, the more he wanted hers. It was a strange switch. He'd deal with it later, though. His first problem was getting her to walk down the aisle, a problem he intended solving immediately.

# *Ten*

Katie had given herself an extra day off, and Phyllis was watching the shop. It was late afternoon when Bill brought his foreman to the house. He introduced her to Sy Baxter, who doffed his cap and firmly shook her hand. A short, wiry man in his middle fifties, he apologized for inconveniencing her. His open face and sparkling brown eyes inspired friendship.

"I'm here to see the job gets done, Katie," he said, repeating Bill's instructions. "I'm to make his Katie happy."

Bill and Katie's gazes met, then slid away as they both recognized new limitations. There would be no stolen moments with Sy in the house. Bill had spent the night in her bed. He'd teased her that it was easier on his knees to make love there than on the bathroom floor. He'd proven it by making exquisite, gentle love to her. That morning they had welcomed the sunrise, then made love again. Each time, Bill used protection.

"Here," Sy added, bringing both of them back to the present. "My missus, Dorothy, wants you to have this for your trouble." He reached into a bag, bringing forth a small wreath of silk flowers for the front door. "She makes these beauties herself," he boasted proudly as Katie thanked him for the lovely present. She liked Bill's foreman.

Upstairs she showed him the room she'd set aside for his use. He quickly yanked his tie off and hung his jacket in the closet. He said he hated dressing up in uncomfortable duds, despised motels and being separated from his missus. "Which ain't often," he added.

Sy, she learned, had fathered five children, all girls, ranging in age from fifteen to twenty-five. He pulled out an accordian of pictures to show Katie.

While Katie dutifully studied each photograph, Sy gazed out the window at the large backyard. "My missus would have enjoyed bringing up our girls in such a lovely house. We live on a lot sixty by eighty. It eliminates mowing. We always intended to move, but one thing led to another and we didn't. You need a hammock between those two elm trees."

"Not a bad idea," Bill agreed.

"Bill, you ought to marry and have a boy we can train to someday run the business."

Sy's unwitting remark brought a distracted look from Bill, who had been thinking more of the boy's mother. "I'm working on it."

"Finish unpacking," Katie said, suddenly self-conscious. "I'm going downstairs to make coffee. Come down when you're ready."

"Don't forget the cookies," Bill called.

"She's cute," Sy said. "Nice lady."

Bill listened to Katie's light step on the stairs. "I know it."

"Is she the one you fixing to marry?"

Bill hooked his thumbs into his belt. "You fixing to mind your business?"

"I wouldn't let her get away," Sy advised, taking advantage of his role as an extended family member.

"I don't intend to. But, Sy, don't say anything to embarrass her."

Katie served coffee and oatmeal-raisin cookies. She nearly upended the platter of cookies when Bill's gaze captured hers with a look of heated intensity. Blushing, she plunged into the history of Cape May, as much for her benefit as for Sy's.

Bill added a bit himself, telling of the band of peace-loving Leni-Lenape Indians who sought relief from the heat at the seashore, and of the New England whalers and rich southern plantation owners.

"We're below the Mason-Dixon line," Katie added, much to her guest's surprise. "We have more Victorian houses here than San Francisco does."

"Are you building a gazebo?" Sy asked. "I see a good spot for it. You can plant roses around its base."

Bill turned to Katie. "Would you like one?"

"That plus a swimming pool," she said, dismissing the idea, although she had always loved gazebos. "The neighbors will think I've hit the jackpot."

"It's none of their business," Bill said. "And I

think we'd get a lot of use out of both a gazebo and a pool."

Sy's gaze shifted from one to the other.

"I'm planning to have offices on both coasts," Bill explained.

Sy nodded, then went on to praise the workmanship and style of the house. "Shouldn't take more than a couple of weeks," he said, sipping his second mug of coffee. " 'Course, it all depends on everyone showing up on time. Don't you worry none, young lady. I'll see to it we clean up the mess as we go along. Bill and I are particular about neatness. We take pride in our work."

"Bill speaks highly of you," Katie said.

"Must be catching. He speaks highly of you too. Has for years. I would have known you anywhere from Bill's description. A tiny redhead, grass-green eyes, and freckles on your nose. He brags about your swimming ability. I understand you've won a good share of trophies. It sure is good to meet you." He winked at Bill. "My Katie."

"My Katie," she teased, amazed that Bill had given Sy so much information about her. "I'm just plain Katie."

"Her name is Katherine Elizabeth," Bill supplied, thinking her anything but plain.

"Katherine Elizabeth, is it? It's a good name."

Bill crossed his arms, staring down at his mug. He didn't appreciate sitting on display like a prize pelican or listening to Sy repeat what he'd told him about Katie. He'd always thought of Katie as his, he realized, with surprised awareness. After all, they had grown up together, he'd taken care of her. She was his, dammit! Now more than ever.

Katherine Elizabeth, he'd learned, was a lusty

wench who prized freedom, almost more than he did. Whenever he'd broached the subject of marriage that day, she veered off in another direction, reminding him to look over their divorce agreement. So far the paper had two items on it. They agreed not to fight; she agreed to unlimited visitation rights. She assured him she'd marry him, then refused to set the date. He was a darn sight more concerned with the visitation rights between the parents at the moment!

He flattened both palms on the tabletop. "Quit blabbing, Sy. Finish your coffee. After we walk the grounds, I want to go over the drawings with you."

Katie bustled about the kitchen after the two men left. For dinner she was going to make a meat loaf, whipped potatoes with a dash of nutmeg, three-bean salad, hot biscuits, and apple pie.

So Bill called her "my Katie." How revealing! She felt a surge of happiness. She intended to take full advantage of Sy's presence. He was a veritable fountain of knowledge.

When the men returned from inspecting the exterior, Bill switched on the television set for Sy, then asked to speak with her. She followed him upstairs to his room, wondering why they couldn't speak in the kitchen. Bill had his hands on his hips and a frown on his face.

"I hope Sy's not going to drive you nuts," he said. "He's a good man, but he's nervous right now. He'll calm down after a bit."

Without thinking, she laid her hands on Bill's chest. "I like Sy. He's a character, but I'm glad he's here. We'll get along."

He covered her hands with his. "What about us?"

She sighed. "We're going to be on our best behavior. It's just as well. Since we're not going to be living together, why get in the habit of making love too often?"

Both moved nearer, as if not to do so would seal a permanent break neither could endure. She had given him her old room. Apart from the new mattress, it hadn't been touched. The wallpaper, a reproduction of the original, repeated a pattern of tiny red roses. In this room Bill had tutored her in geometry and coached her in spelling. She'd won the school's spelling bee. He had also nailed a banner above her maple bed, a banner that proclaimed her state spelling champion. Above the desk were two shelves containing her swimming trophies.

Katie slipped past him to open the hope chest at the foot of the bed. She placed an extra blanket on top of the counterpane.

"Stay warm tonight, Bill."

"I'd prefer to stay warm with you," he said. "I wish I hadn't asked Sy to come. I don't want to sleep alone."

"Get used to it, darling. If you're very lonely, I'll send Samson for company."


Work on Katie's house began the next day. Although she had confidence in Sy, and assuredly in Bill, she remained home in the morning in case they needed her to help make decisions. When she arrived at work after lunch, she smiled at the sight of the newly installed carpeting.

Sweet Mischief looked as if it had undergone a face lift. The carpeting blended perfectly with the walls. Sprigs of flowers in small vases brightened the candy displays.

"Sorry I'm late," she said to Phyllis. "What a difference the new carpeting makes. I love it."

"How was Atlantic City?" Phyllis asked. "Did anything special happen?"

"The weather was wonderful. We ate cones of spun sugar, had chili dogs on the boardwalk, went swimming, saw a dinner show, and danced the Lambada."

Phyllis rolled her eyes. "Do I have to drag it out of you?"

"Are you asking me if we made love?"

"I wasn't going to put it so bluntly, but yes."

"We did. But only because of his malaria."

"Malaria!" Phyllis screeched. "What are you talking about? Does Bill have malaria?"

"No, he tricked me."

Phyllis sat down heavily. "Katie, I'm not as young as I used to be. Run this by me again. Slowly."

When Katie got to the part about the ice cubes, Phyllis held her stomach, she was laughing so hard. "Goodness!" she howled. "You two are crazy. Now what?"

"Bill pretended to have malaria so I would keep him warm," Katie said dreamily.

Phyllis shook her head. "You fell for one of the oldest ploys in the book."

"No, I didn't. It didn't work. He confessed. Bill's an honest scoundrel."

"Katie, I realize that you and Bill are having one of the most unorthodox courtships I've ever heard of, but where do you stand now? Has he told you he loves you?"

Katie's romantic illusions faded. "No. I'm guilty of sins of the flesh, I suppose. I don't know what to do. Last night I asked Bill how much the remodeling and restoring of my house would cost. At first he refused to answer, but I pressed him until he told me."

"What's on your mind?"

"If he doesn't love me, I intend to pay him for the work."

"How? You haven't the money."

"I'll sell the house."

"You love your house!" Phyllis cried. "Where would you go if you sold it? You talked your parents into selling it to you in the first place, so that when they visit, they visit you and their memories. Katie, think again. You'd hate leaving your Victorian, and you know it."

She would. Katie wanted to huddle into a ball and cry. Instead she put up a brave front. "Bill and I never stuck to the rules I made. I couldn't. He wouldn't. The man never quits. You'd be surprised at the things he's done."

Frustrated, she drove her fingers through her hair and marched into the bathroom. She combed her hair, then dabbed water on her burning eyes.

"Are you sorry, Katie?" Phyllis asked when she returned. "About everything, I mean?"

Katie's shoulders drooped in defeat. How could she lie? "No, I'm not sorry we made love. Yes, I'm miserable. It's very confusing. We fight, but can't keep away from each other. It's awful."

Phyllis picked a few dead leaves off the African violets she'd set near a display of chocolate-covered cherries. "You're daft. Didn't you promise to marry him?"

Katie sniffled. "Yes, but I thought I could change his attitude. I can't. We had a discussion about his feelings toward divorce. When I saw I was getting nowhere, I told him we were so friendly we'd enjoy our divorce."

They fell silent as several customers came in the shop. At the next lull, Phyllis asked, "How did he take it?"

"Not well. He wants us to marry immediately."

"There, you see. Everything's wonderful."

"You know why," Katie said glumly. "Don't forget about Bill's knees. I feel like I'm a tightrope walker. I don't think I should marry him."

She blew out a gusty breath and picked up a cloth. She needed to work off steam. While Phyllis watched in sympathy, Katie dusted. She washed shelves that already sparkled. She rearranged neat file drawers. She emptied and refilled trays of candy.

She waited on customers. She pored over mail-order catalogs. She phoned suppliers and placed ads announcing her mail-order business.

"What are you trying to prove?" Phyllis asked several hours later.

Katie opened a box of paper clips. "It helps to keep busy."

"It's time you settled this in your mind, before you drive yourself and me crazy."

Katie leaned both elbows on her desk. "I'm listening."

"Katie, are you in love with Bill?"

She nodded.

"You wanted a courtship?"

She nodded again. "And romance."

"Marry him. Don't wait for utopia. Don't be miserable the rest of your life."

"I'm going to be miserable anyway. I told you, Phil, the sooner Bill and I marry, the sooner he gets his freedom. I'm tired of pretending that's what I want. I'd rather not marry."

"Are you sure?"

"No," Katie said glumly. "I'm not sure of anything lately."

"Don't quit," Phyllis advised. "If you do, I won't let you be godmother to this baby."

Thankfully business picked up again, taking Katie's mind off her troubles. It was only when she returned home that she hauled up her brave front again, hiding her true feelings from Bill as she sought to decide what to do about her future.

During the rest of the week they developed a routine. She prepared dinner while Bill set the table. Without admitting it, each savored this brief time alone, permitting themselves a casual caress or a quickly shared kiss. The downside was that each wanted more. At dinner, Sy did most of the talking. Afterward Bill excused himself to go upstairs to his room, and for the next several hours, he conducted his business via the telephone.

As the days progressed, Katie grew used to the sounds of electric tools and sanding machines. In the dining room a large plastic bag protected the chandelier. Fresh plaster covered the walls. Wallpaper arrived for the bathrooms and the vestibule. New moldings skirted the ceiling in the parlor. The mullioned windows were releaded. A carpenter hauled away the old porch, a new one took its place. Painters scraped and prepared the exterior of her house.

At the end of the second week, Bill left the house before Katie awoke. She had no idea where he'd gone. Nor did Sy. Missing his companionship at breakfast, she drove to work earlier than usual. She toyed with the idea of going home for lunch, then gave it up as Phyllis insisted on discussing the new advertising campaign. When Bill walked into the store late in the afternoon, her heart tripped with pleasure. He wore jeans, an old shirt, and a brown leather jacket.

"Hi, there," she said.

He greeted Phyllis, then said to Katie, "We've got an errand to go on."

She looked at him questioningly, but he only smiled and led her toward the closet for her coat. "Where are we going?" she asked.

"Phyllis," he said, "tell this girl it's time we picked out an engagement ring."

For several seconds Katie and Bill stared at each other. With a glint in his eye, he wrapped his arms about her. "Come on, Katie. Phyllis, Katie says good-bye."

Katie offered a feeble protest. "I can't. It's too early for me to leave."

Phyllis shooed her out. "Get going, Katie, and remember my advice."

Sitting in Bill's car, she watched as he passed first one, then another jewlery store, until they'd driven outside of town. "Where are you taking me?"

He kept his eyes straight ahead. "You'll see."

"Bill, I hate surprises."

He grinned at her. "Liar."

He drove to Higbee's Beach, commonly known as Diamond Beach, now deserted on a winter's afternoon. He stopped the car, then came around to her side to open the door.

"It's a lovely day for a picnic, isn't it?" he said.

A hawk and a seagull circled overhead. Waves gently lapped the shoreline.

Katie laughed. "You nut. You're barely over your attack of malaria. Is this the big surprise?"

He waved his hand in an arc. "This is the jewelry store, Katie. It's open late, as you can see."

They were on a rock-strewn beach where many of the pure quartz pebbles had been ground into smooth shapes over millions of years. When cut and polished, the stones resembled various colored diamonds. Jewelers crafted the stones into rings, necklaces, and pins.

"What are you doing?" she asked, as Bill lifted something from the trunk of the car.

"I'm getting the rest of the equipment. We could be here indefinitely. It may take weeks to find the right stone."

"You're a big sport," she said. They'd collected Cape May diamonds all their lives. "We'll freeze to death first."

"I doubt it. It's still fairly warm." He threw a blanket down on the beach, then set up a tripod with a brazier on top. He shook a layer of charcoal briquettes into it, lit a match, and had a fire going.

Katie watched in amusement.

"You never can tell if we'll be shipwrecked," he said, going back to the car. "Here, put these on,

Katie." He handed her a package. In it were a pair of woolen slacks, a sweater, her boots, and socks.

"Where should I change?" she asked, beginning to feel giddy.

He scrutinized the ribbons of pebbles stretching outward to the water's edge. "In the absence of a cave, I suggest the car."

She questioned his sanity but did as he asked, letting his happy mood infect her. In contrast to her skirt and blouse, the warm clothes felt good in the cooling air. Bill looked her over. His eyes told her he liked what he saw.

He tossed her a child's shovel and sand bucket. "Start digging. Find a pretty engagement pebble, Katie."

"Thanks," she said drolly. "What are you going to do?"

"I'm going to find a stick and roast marshmallows. I seem to remember you cheated me out of my marshmallows. You dig," he said pleasantly. "I'll eat."

"And if I say no?" she asked, grinning.

He sauntered over to her. "I'd call you a spoilsport, which is about what I expected from you. I suppose I'll have to crawl graciously on my poor knees and help you. After we eat."

She stuck out her tongue.

He roasted the marshmallows, making a big ceremony of pulling the sweet from the stick. They sucked the sugary concoction, outlining their mouths with gooey drippings. "No more," Bill said at last. "It's time to dig."

Katie fell into the spirit of the game. They poked around the rocks, hunting like excited kids, vying for the prize in a Cracker Jack box.

They sifted through odd and round-shaped stones, searching for the colorless quartz that when dipped in water became bright and shiny. These were the Cape May diamonds. Katie found a yellow quartz; Bill found a green one. Neither found the colorless variety.

Finally Katie brushed her knees and sat back on her haunches. Her face and eyes sparkled. "This jewelry store is fresh out of diamonds, Bill. We'll have to use a cigar band."

His knees creaking, he helped her up. She carried the bucket and shovel back to the car, happy for the unexpected outing.

She felt his breath on her neck as he came up behind her. He pivoted her to face him. "I don't smoke, so I guess I'll have to give you this."

Her gaze flew to his face, remaining riveted there as he placed a blue velvet ring box in her hand.

"Open it, Katherine Elizabeth," he said huskily.

She put down the shovel and bucket and brushed the sand from her hands before lifting the lid of the box. In its velvet folds nestled a marquise-cut diamond solitaire. Her heart pounded absurdly fast.

"You said you wanted romance, Katie."

She raised her head. He lowered his. He placed a long reverent kiss on her lips, then rested his fingertips on her cheeks, gazing into her eyes.

"It's beautiful," she breathed. "It fits perfectly."

"I borrowed one of your rings so the jeweler could size it properly."

"Bill, this isn't necessary."

"I want you to have it. Katie, let's marry right away."

"All right," she heard herself agree. She'd wanted romance. Bill had given her romance. He'd also arranged for the wedding. He hadn't once said he loved her.

She swallowed her hurt. Bill couldn't be blamed for acting like himself. It was she who must compromise. Her gaze strayed to the ring on her finger. How long would she have the right to wear it? she wondered.

When they arrived home in the fading light, he led her to the backyard. Before turning the corner into it, he blindfolded her eyes with his hands. She sensed his excitement.

"All right," he said. "You can look now."

He took his hands away. "How do you like it?"

Katie was speechless. Somehow, in the space of a day's time, a miracle had transformed her yard. It no longer looked plain and drab in its winter coat. The bare branches of the trees blazed with tiny lights. Off to the side was a hexagon-shaped pink gazebo. Anchored in its center in full view, was a huge urn filled with colorful balloons. Between two elm trees hung a large hammock.

"You can sit in the gazebo and watch our son," Bill said proudly. "I thought we'd wait to build the pool until he's older, and it's safe. What do you think, Katie?"

Sy came around the house to where they stood. "Bill near burst his seams," he said, "waiting to show this to you. He snuck in the carpenters and the painters the minute you left for work today. If you don't like pink, we'll paint it whatever color you want. He said you're gonna love it."

She looked from one to the other, at Sy's beaming face, at Bill's filled with eager anticipation.

She touched the diamond solitaire that Bill had given her, not in love, but in grateful acknowledgment of her keeping her part of the bargain. She surrendered to the awful knowledge that she wouldn't go back on her word. She was going to marry a man who didn't love her.

"That's the reason I didn't want you home too early today," Bill said, hugging her close. "Well?"

She caught her breath. "I'm speechless."

Sy poked Bill's arm. "See, what did I tell you?"

"Honey, we don't have to wait until we finish the upstairs for the housewarming party. I've got to leave for a few days. When I return, the downstairs should be completed. Sy'll make sure, won't you, Sy?"

"You bet."

Bile rose in Katie's throat.

"We'll have the old gang over, Katie. Would you like that?" Bill gazed at her raptly, waiting for her to give permission. Unable to speak, she bobbed her head like a cork.

Then she burst into tears and fled toward the house as though her life were at stake.

"Just like a woman," Sy clucked. "Don't you worry none, Bill. She's happy is all. Heck, with the ring and the gazebo and now a party to plan, it's only natural she's overwhelmed. Trust me, all women cry when they're happy."

# *Eleven*

---

Katie sprinted out of the yard and around the corner of the house, startling a painter cleaning his paintbrush. She shunned Bill's entreaties to stop. Swinging open the door, she flew up the stairs to her bedroom, scaring Samson, who lay curled in a ball on the top step. She threw herself onto the bed, her mood devastated by Bill's largesse.

The more he gave, the worse she felt.

Bill followed close on her heels. When he saw her lying on the bed, crying, he brought a chair up and sat. He gently touched her hair, stroked her back, trying to ease her wrenching sobs.

"Hush now, Katie. It can't be that bad."

She flopped over onto her back and stared up at him. His engagement ring shone on her finger. She sniffled. "I suppose you want to elope right away?"

"Sy thinks you're crying because you're happy."

"A lot he knows," she mumbled.

Bill handed her a tissue. "Better not tell him. He thinks all women cry when they're happy."

She watched uneasily as Bill's mouth curved in a wry grin. With his index finger he lightly traced a path up her arm and across her shoulder to her neck.

"Was it the party or the gazebo that threw you for a loop?" he asked.

She turned away. "The party didn't help."

He handed her another tissue. "You don't like giving parties," he joked, but his eyes were serious.

"It depends on the reason for giving a party."

He held her hands, rubbing his thumb over the ring. "Do you trust me?"

"Not especially."

He tried more teasing. "Afraid of my malaria?"

"No, of your knees."

Something flickered in his expression, then disappeared. "My knees?"

She tossed her head on the pillow and gave vent to her pent-up frustration. "Figure it out for yourself."

He tightened his lips. "I'm trying. Humor me, Katie. Are you crying out of happiness or abject misery?"

She hedged her answer, knowing once the words left her lips there'd be no turning back. Phyllis would claim she was out of her mind. In time she'd think so too. Bill was the only man in the world for her.

She sighed. "A little of both."

He stopped beating around the bush. "Do you want to call it off?"

She bit her lip. How should she tell the man she loved she couldn't marry him? Should she come out with it and say, sorry? Or should she try to lessen the hurt? Should she tell him before his engagement ring welded to her finger?

"Katie?"

"I think we should wait."

"Why?" he asked in disbelief.

"Because I'm afraid."

Confused, he asked, "Of what?" It was the one answer he had not anticipated. He felt empty and lost and very unsure of himself. If he were to be honest, he'd admit he was scared too. He tried to imagine what he'd done to trigger fear in her.

"Answer me, Katie."

She threw her legs over the side of the bed and hoisted herself up in honorable resignation. She flung open the closet, dragged out a suitcase, and tossed it onto her bed. "I don't even know where to begin. You're a very generous man. I'm an ungrateful woman. Those are facts. Another fact is that I can't help myself."

"Katie, gratitude has nothing to do with this. What are you doing?"

Anguished, she gazed at his dear face. Her throat clogged with tears. "Right now I'm no use to anybody. I'm going away for a few days. I need to be alone to get back my sanity."

"Your sanity? An hour ago we were having fun at the beach, roasting marshmallows. I gave you an engagement ring. If anyone is losing sanity, it's me."

She went to her dresser, opening her lingerie drawer. "You're probably right," she said, gaining the courage to speak. "Tell the workmen to go home. I'll pay for whatever costs you've incurred.

I want out. I thought I could go through with it, but I can't. Not even for you."

She removed the engagement ring and dropped it into his palm. "I appreciate the ring, and how you gave it to me and all. I do. Someday you'll find a woman who will be thrilled to give you the son you want. I can't. Sy will be happy to go home, I'm sure. He loves being with his wife and daughters. His marriage isn't a sham. He didn't buy his neighbor's house as a retreat."

She tossed a week's supply of underwear into her suitcase. "You almost made me change my mind."

Bill looked stunned. "And now you've suddenly seen the light?"

Her shoulders lifted and fell. "Bill, I've always seen the light. I didn't want to acknowledge my feelings. I chose to ignore them. I wanted to pretend."

She saw him carefully bank his anger. Her gaze lingered on his hair, still wet from the ocean spray, his hands that had slipped the ring on her finger, his blue eyes dulled now with shock. She loved him, but she couldn't have him, not on his terms.

"Bill," she went on in a choked voice, "I never meant to hurt you or mislead you. You never lied to me or pretended feelings you don't have." She gulped back a knot of emotion. She couldn't continue. She bent over, rocking in silent misery, tension cramping her stomach.

"Would you please leave?" Her tears were flowing freely again, and when Bill disregarded her request, gathering her in his arms instead, it felt so good, she cried even harder, dampening his shirt.

He sighed wearily, sadly. Tilting her head up, he gazed at her tear-streaked face. "I guess I really didn't know you after all, did I, Katie?"

"You knew me as a child, Bill. I knew you as a boy. We're adults now. We've changed. I'm sorry."

"How can you say that?" he argued. "We were two adults that night in Atlantic City. What about the other night?"

"As you said, 'Adults engage in recreational sex.' "

"Funny," he said, his tone etched with biting sarcasm. "You didn't seem the type. Shows you what I know."

She freed herself and turned her back, unable to bear his mockery.

"About the house," he said coldly. "I hired the workmen for the job on short notice, guaranteeing them work. Let them stay and finish, Katie. Don't worry about the money."

Talk of money and obligations devastated her more than if Bill had stormed out of her room. She stumbled toward the door. Bill made a strangled sound in his throat and caught her to him. As he stroked her hair, he voiced the fear that had been growing inside him.

"Katie, is it that you think a baby will mean the end of your freedom?"

Filled with remorse, she voiced her hopelessness. "Yes, that's it, Bill," she lied.

The lie had the desired effect. Bill dropped his hands from her, taking with him his warmth and comfort. He stood silent for a long time. "That's it, then," he said finally, harshly.

She had lost him as friend and as lover. "Good-bye, Bill."

When she turned away, she saw his ring lying on her pillow.

"What have I done?" she muttered.


Like many who cause cataclysmic ruptures in their lives, Katie settled into a period of withering self-doubt. She alternated between resignation and affirmation, convincing herself she'd acted wisely in calling off her marriage to Bill. She told herself it wouldn't have been fair to him to keep her feelings hidden.

She never did go away for a few days as she wanted to. Sweet Mischief needed her. It wouldn't have been fair to Phyllis, nor did she have money to spare. Despite Bill's offer to pay for the restoration, Katie kept careful records. Unlike Bill, the local workmen weren't shy about telling her their fees. They were astronomical. She calculated it would take her years to repay Bill.

Sy checked into a motel the day Bill left. She told him he didn't have to go. He thanked her but refused.

Phyllis wisely refrained from casting blame on Katie, proving the quality of their friendship. As always the women began their day by sharing coffee and a bagel. To Katie, the coffee tasted like mud; the bagel, dry paper. Although she politely asked about Phyllis's son, Charlie, her mind wandered through the answer. Katie passed many days in a haze.

Ironically, her mail-order business received a boost when several catalog ads earned big dividends. A woman contacted her to purchase candies for a hotel chain. They drew up a year's contract. In another instance, Katie bid on a contract that supplied fund-raising gifts to charities. She approached a manufacturer who was also a friend, convincing him that half a loaf was better than none.

While her business slowly increased, her house returned to its former majesty. It had new bargeboards, elaborately carved and decorated, and a watertight roof, guaranteed by its manufacturer to last twenty-five years. Katie wondered morosely if she'd last twenty-five years. Without Bill, she doubted she'd last five.

With the temperature holding in the upper fifties, the painters finished the exterior work. The new driveway and the wainscotting in the dining room and parlor were completed. New appliances gleamed in the kitchen. Katie had tried to cancel the order, only to be informed that Mr. Logan had already paid.

Distressed by the increasing amount of money she felt she owed Bill, Katie beseeched Sy to tell her how to get in touch with him. She and Sy were on friendly terms. He hated seeing her despair. Unaware of the true reason for Bill's sudden departure, he assumed they'd simply had a lover's spat. Katie refrained from telling him that she had been the one to send Bill away.

"If he's not in his office, Katie, he's in the field. He could be anywhere."

Janice floated into the store one Wednesday. She let Katie know that she had dined with Bill the previous night. Katie covered her surprise and her hurt. She hadn't known Bill had returned.

When she mentioned it to Phyllis, she realized from her reaction her friend had known. She missed Bill terribly. It was a wound incapable of healing. At night, to relieve the quiet in her bedroom, she kept the radio on for comfort. She slept fitfully, awakening often to remember their love-making.

On Sunday, when the late-afternoon sun slanted across the dining-room floor and the crystal chandelier cast rainbows on the walls, Katie heard an automobile horn outside. For a moment she half hoped it might be Bill. Glancing out the glass door, though, she saw Phyllis walking up the path.

"Hi, what brings you here?" Katie asked. "Don't you see enough of me in the store?"

Phyllis lumbered past her into the kitchen and sat. "I could use a cup of tea if you don't mind."

Katie filled the teakettle.

"Bill's in town. What are you going to do about it?"

Operating on a short fuse, Katie bristled. "Is that why you're here? You know I'm aware that Bill's in town. Janice couldn't wait to tell me she'd had dinner with him. So you see, Bill's recovered nicely. He invested a little time, but I gave him his money's worth."

Phyllis studied her sympathetically. Unlike her usual lively self, Katie was pale and exhausted most days. "I used to think you were smart. Bill didn't ask Janice to dinner, contrary to the barracuda's information. They ran into each other in the restaurant. Janice moved to his table."

"Whatever the reason, nothing's changed." Katie

wouldn't admit she was glad Bill hadn't dated Janice.

"How come he's back?" Phyllis asked.

Katie pressed her lips together, drawing on reserves of strength to keep from yelling at her friend. Lately she'd been jumpy and out of sorts. She knew the reason, hoped it might pass. It hadn't. She missed Bill with every nerve in her body. She missed his humor. She missed the spontaneity between them. The prospect of losing her friendship with Phyllis, too, was more than she could imagine.

She purposely held her temper in check. "Phyllis, I'd appreciate it if you'd drop the subject. I'm fine. Everything is wonderful. Go home."

Phyllis stirred her tea. "Wrong. You're not fine. You look like hell. Your skin's too pale even for a redhead. Katie, there's no turning back. Too much has changed. You're miserable to be around. I don't like it. It's bad for my baby for his mother to be tense."

Katie crumpled. Nothing she did or said when it came to her loved ones was right anymore.

"Has Fred told you to quit?" she asked.

"He's suggested it. It has nothing to do with you. He thinks I ought to be home with my time so near."

Katie sighed and put her hand on Phyllis's shoulder. "He's right, you know. I'll ask Sally to start right away."

"I'd feel a lot better if you called Bill, Katie. No one is awarded medals for suffering."

Bill listened to Sy's report. When he was through,

he asked, "How much longer until you're through over there?"

"We're practically finished. A day or two more," Sy replied. "I tell you the house is a cheerless wonder since you and Katie broke up. She doesn't know I hear her, but she cries a lot. Samson's not cheering her up either."

Bill could have told Sy he needed cheering too. He'd flown to Arizona to meet with his new clients. During the entire time he met with them, his mind was on Katie. Matters didn't improve when he flew to Palm Springs to see his parents.

"Son, what's wrong?" his father had asked. They were taking a walk after dinner.

Bill had confided his whole messed-up plan to have a son.

"No wonder Katie threw you out!" his father exclaimed. "That sweet girl. What you put her through!"

Bill was not in the best of humor. With a pessimistic certainty his life was going to be hell without Katie, he feebly defended his actions. "She put me through hell. Whose side are you on?"

"Hers," his father replied rapidly, "and yours too. Better not repeat a word of this to your mother. She'll have your hide. We love Katie like a daughter. She's family. Son, you'd best ask yourself why you're so miserable. Heck, if this were a pure business deal you wouldn't be torturing yourself. You've had deals sour. We all have. Seems to me you're having a powerful reaction to this business proposition."

Bill had the nagging suspicion his father was right. Life without Katie vacillated between miserable and miserably awful. He missed her laugh, her smile, her teasing, her loving. He dreamed of their time together.

"Examine your heart, son," his father advised. "You'll find the answer there."

In a flash of clear insight, he acknowledged his reason for insisting on completing Katie's house was to maintain contact with her, one way or the other. It had nothing to do with a baby, but everything to do with the baby's mother.

He couldn't give up Katie.

He wasn't thinking about a son.

He wanted Katie.

With or without children.

He loved her.

He couldn't live without her.

Bill left the following day for Cape May.

The answer, when he listened to his heart, was simple. He'd been in love with her all his life. She was the reason no other woman could ever mean anything to him, why he found each one lacking. It had been Katie from the start.

Now he needed to convince Katie that he loved her for herself.

"Sy," he said, bringing his attention back to the present, "I want to thank you for looking after Katie for me."

"I didn't do anything," he said.

Bill smiled. "I'm about to ask you to do something out of the ordinary, a bit out of your regular line of work."

Sy looked dubious.

"Your missus would approve, Sy," Bill cajoled.

Hearing Bill's plan, Sy agreed—after he stopped laughing!

Bill dragged Sy with him to the library. They

searched through books until Bill found what he needed. Leaving the library, he and Sy went shopping.

"It's got to be authentic," Bill informed a sales clerk. He handed him a photocopied page of a library book. "Here's what I need."

"Shouldn't I be working until you need me?" Sy asked as the clerk found what Bill needed.

"You're working now. I need your support," Bill said.

"How's Katie going to know the difference about this stuff?"

Bill tucked his package beneath his arm. "Katie will know. Trust me."

Sy scratched his chin. "If it was me, I'd drag her off by the hair. Women like that."

"Are you saying you dragged your wife off by her hair?" Bill asked.

"Nope. Never had to." His wink told Bill he was teasing.

Bill placed a phone call to Phyllis. "Keep Katie at the store until I give you the all clear."

"How do you propose I do that?" Phyllis asked.

"I don't know."

"Are you in love with her?"

"Desperately," he said truthfully. "I can't eat, sleep, or concentrate."

"Then I'll help. It's about time you came to your senses. I hope it works."

"So do I."

He and Sy drove to Katie's house, which sparkled gracefully under a fresh coat of paint and a new roof. Bill parked his car in the garage, glad for once that she had a habit of leaving her own car in the driveway. After he and Sy hauled his packages into the house, Bill made a thorough inspection of the interior. "You and the men did a fine job."

Sy nodded, accepting the praise modestly.

"I hope the delivery man gets here soon," he said.

As if on cue, the doorbell rang. Bill quickly paid for the bulky purchase and turned to Sy.

"Okay, let's set it up," he said.

"You sure this is necessary?" Sy asked. He stepped back and laughed.

"Come on, dammit. We don't have all day."

When they finished, the men congratulated each other.

"Okay," Bill said, "you're off the hook. Thanks for helping. And if you breathe one word of this, you're fired."

Laughing, Sy wished Bill luck.

Bill phoned Phyllis and told her he was ready. All he could do now was wait and pray.

Still wondering at Phyllis's insistence they discuss offering a new flavor of fudge until half an hour after closing time, Katie let herself in the house. The first thing that struck her as odd was the music. The second thing that struck her was that the kitten hadn't met her at the door. Deciding the workers had left the radio on, she followed the sound into the parlor. The sight greeting her literally took her breath away.

"I don't believe it!" she screeched.

All of the furniture—the sofa, two end tables, the floor lamp, three armchairs, a magazine rack, the spinet and bench—lined the sides of the room. The disconnected telephone sat atop a table.

In the center of the room, its pole reaching almost to the high ceiling, was a leather tepee. Samson was busily tugging on one of its base strings. "Get lost, Samson," Bill hissed.

Katie held a hand over her mouth to keep from whooping. She'd know Bill's hiss anywhere. "Samson, who's in there?" she asked.

No answer.

"I'll just have to call the police, won't I?"

"Don't you dare!" a voice boomed.

She'd recognize Bill's voice anywhere.

Katie peeked inside. Bill sat cross-legged on the floor inside the tepee. He wore a loin cloth and full head regalia. On his feet were beaded moccasins.

Her heart hammered in her breast. She hadn't minded staying late at the store, knowing she was coming home to an empty house. Yet, on the drive home, a strong feeling had come over her. She hadn't been able to identify its source. All she knew was that she needed to be home as quickly as possible. Now she knew why.

"Passing through," she asked, "or is this a raid?"

"I came to smoke the peace pipe," Bill said, his eyes a dusky blue.

"Do you smoke it alone or can anyone join you?" she asked, coming inside. She looked down at him, at his knobby knees. She gazed into his eyes and saw his love.

"I love you, Katie," he said, telling her what she yearned to hear. "I've always loved you. I was too dumb and too frightened by other peoples' mistakes to realize that what we have is rare."

Reaching out, he brought her down to him. "Please love me. I can't live without you. My father won't forgive me unless you do. My mother wants you for her daughter-in-law. My uncle John is angry with me, and he doesn't know the reason why. He simply agrees with my folks. Sy advised me to drag you to the altar by the hair. He said that's what I should do if my method fails."

"He did, did he?" she said softly.

"Yes," Bill replied, too anxious to play games.

"And what is your method?"

"The truth," he muttered thickly. "A truth it took me too many years to learn. I love you. I only pray it isn't too late."

She smiled with happiness. "In that case, shouldn't we be making up?"

He covered her lips with his, drinking from her the taste he held so dear. "God, how I've missed you. I'd move," he said, "but I've been down here so long I don't think I can."

She kissed his knees. "Bill, why are you in a tepee in the middle of my living room, dressed like an Indian?"

Kissing her, he took a long time until he answered. "Do you remember the story I told you about Chief Seattle?"

"Mmmm. Kiss me there again," she demanded. Bill dutifully lifted her hair to the side, kissing her neck. She shivered deliciously. "And there." He complied.

"Oooh . . . yes, there."

Bill very nearly forgot his story.

"Chief Seattle had brains," he finally said. "When he spoke about the importance of the circle and leaving your seed to the next generation,

I missed his most vital message. It's the essence of his teaching. He wasn't a chauvinist. I believe he meant the circle is a man and a woman. We're life's most important link. You and I, Katie. We forge the circle. You're more important to me than anything or anyone."

"Even a son?" she asked.

"Even a son," he replied solemnly. "Katie, do you love me?"

With the last barrier down, she answered with her heart. "I always have. I loved when you wouldn't wait three days to kiss me. I loved you when you nearly died of malaria. I loved you when you made love to me in Atlantic City. I loved you on the bathroom floor. I loved you in my bed."

He kissed her full on the lips. "Do you think you could manage to love me in a tepee?"

"Is this a proposal of marriage?"

"If it isn't, I'm making a fool of myself."

"Say it nicely."

"Katherine Elizabeth Reynolds, will you please marry me? I love you madly, dearly, and I hope—intimately."

"I accept, darling. Are you wearing anything beneath that loin cloth?" she asked mischievously.

He smiled. His fingers coiled in her hair, his lips claimed her mouth. This was his Katie, his for the rest of his life. His gaze traveled to her breasts, their outline just visible under the chiffon blouse she wore. His hands traveled up her thigh.

"What do you think?" he whispered.

She moaned. When he touched her like that she could hardly speak. "I think we'd better find out before your knees age any more. Or if you prefer, I can invite our friends in for a powwow. You said you wanted a party."

"Not dressed in this I don't."

"What a pity. You have such nice knees."

"We'll make our own party," he said, and started the festivities.

# THE EDITOR'S CORNER

What could be more romantic—Valentine's Day and six LOVESWEPT romances all in one glorious month. And I have the great pleasure of writing my first editor's corner. Let me introduce myself: My name is Nita Taublib, and I have worked as an editorial consultant with the Loveswept staff since Loveswept began. As Carolyn is on vacation and Susann is still at home with her darling baby daughter, I have the honor of introducing the fabulous reading treasures we have in store for you. February is a super month for LOVESWEPT!

Deborah Smith's heroes are always fascinating, and in **THE SILVER FOX AND THE RED-HOT DOVE,** LOVESWEPT #450, the mysterious T. S. Audubon is no exception. He is intrigued by the shy Russian woman who accompanies a famous scientist to a party. And he finds himself filled with a desire to help her escape from her keepers! But when Elena Petrovic makes her own desperate escape, she is too terrified to trust him. Could her handsome enigmatic white-haired rescuer be the silver fox of her childhood fantasy, the only man who could set her loose from a hideous captivity, or does he plan to keep her for himself? Mystery and romance are combined in this passionate tale that will move you to tears.

What man could resist having a gorgeous woman as a bodyguard? Well, as Gail Douglas shows in **BANNED IN BOSTON,** LOVESWEPT #451, rugged and powerful Matt Harper never expects a woman to show up when his mother hires a security consultant to protect him after he receives a series of threatening letters. Annie Brentwood is determined to prove that the best protection de-

*(continued)*

mands brains, not brawn. But she forgets that she must also protect herself from the shameless, arrogant, and oh-so-male Matt, who finds himself intoxicated and intrigued by her feisty spirit. Annie finds it hard to resist a man who promises her the last word and I guarantee you will find this a hard book to put down.

Patt Bucheister's hero in **TROPICAL STORM,** LOVESWEPT #452, will make your temperature rise to sultry heights as he tries to woo Cass Mason. Wyatt Brodie has vowed to take Cass back to Key West for a reconciliation with her desperately ill mother. He challenges her to face her past, promising to help if she'll let him. Can she dare surrender to the hunger he has ignited in her yearning heart? Wyatt has warned her that once he makes love to her, they can never be just friends, that he'll fight to keep her from leaving the island. Can he claim the woman he's branded with the fire of his need? Don't miss this very touching, very emotional story.

From the sunny, sultry South we move to snowy Denver in **FROM THIS DAY FORWARD,** LOVESWEPT #453, by Joan Elliot Pickart. John-Trevor Payton has been assigned to befriend Paisley Kane to discover if sudden wealth and a reunion with the father she's never known will bring her happiness or despair. When Paisley knocks John-Trevor into a snowdrift and falls into his arms, his once firmly frozen plans for eternal bachelorhood begin to melt. Paisley has surrounded herself with a patchwork family of nutty boarders in her Denver house, and John-Trevor envies the pleasure she gets from the people she cares for. But Paisley fears she must choose between a fortune and the man destined to

*(continued)*

be hers. Don't miss this wonderful romance—a real treat for the senses!

Helen Mittermeyer weaves another fascinating story of two lovers reunited in **THE MASK,** LOVE-SWEPT #455. When Cas Griffith lost his young bride to a plane crash over Nepal he was full of grief and guilt and anger. He believed he'd never again want a woman as he'd desired Margo, but when he comes face-to-face with the exotic, mysterious T'ang Qi in front of a New York art gallery two years later, he feels his body come to life again—and knows he must possess the artist who seems such an unusual combination of East and West. The reborn love discovered through their suddenly intimate embraces stuns them both as they seek to exorcise the ghosts of past heartbreak with a love that knows the true meaning of forever.

Sandra Chastain's stories fairly sizzle with powerful emotion and true love, and for this reason we are thrilled to bring you **DANNY'S GIRL,** LOVE-SWEPT #454. Katherine Sinclair had found it hard to resist the seductive claim Danny Dark's words had made on her heart when she was seventeen. Danny had promised to meet her after graduation, but he never came, leaving her to face a pregnancy alone. She'd given the baby up for adoption, gone to college, ended up mayor of Dark River, and never heard from Danny again . . . until now. Has he somehow discovered that she was raising her son, Mike—their son—now that his adoptive parents had died? Has he returned merely to try to take Mike from her? Danny still makes her burn and ache with a sizzling passion, but once they know the truth about the past, they have to discover if it is love or only memory that has lasted.

*(continued)*

Katherine longs to show him that they are a family, that the only time she'll ever be happy is in his arms. You won't soon forget this story of two people and their son trying to become a family.

I hope that you enjoy each and every one of these Valentine treats. We've got a great year of reading pleasure in store for you. . . .

Sincerely,

*Nita Taublib*

Nita Taublib,
Editorial Consultant,
*LOVESWEPT*
Bantam Books
666 Fifth Avenue
New York, NY 10103

## *Starting in February . . .*

An exciting,
unprecedented
mass market
publishing program
designed just for
you . . .
and the way you buy
books!

Over the past few years, the popularity of genre authors has been unprecedented. Their success is no accident, because readers like you demand high levels of quality from your authors and reward them with fierce loyalty.

Now Bantam Books, the foremost English language mass market publisher in the world, takes another giant step in leadership by dedicating the majority of its paperback list to six genre imprints each and every month.

The six imprints that you will see wherever books are sold are:

## SPECTRA.

*For five years the premier publisher of science fiction and fantasy. Now Spectra expands to add one title to its list each month, a horror novel.*

## CRIME LINE.

*The award-winning imprint of crime and mystery fiction. Crime Line will expand to embrace even more areas of contemporary suspense.*

## DOMAIN.

*An imprint that consolidates Bantam's dominance in the frontier fiction, historical saga, and traditional Western markets.*

## FALCON.

*High-tech action, suspense, espionage, and adventure novels will all be found in the Falcon imprint, along with Bantam's successful Air & Space and War books.*

## BANTAM NONFICTION.

*A wide variety of commercial nonfiction, including true crime, health and nutrition, sports, reference books . . . and much more*

## AND NOW IT IS OUR SPECIAL PLEASURE TO INTRODUCE TO YOU THE SIXTH IMPRINT

# FANFARE

TM

FANFARE is the showcase for Bantam's popular women's fiction. With spectacular covers and even more spectacular stories. FANFARE presents three novels each month—ranging from historical to contemporary—all with great human emotion, all with great love stories at their heart, all by the finest authors writing in any genre.

**FANFARE LAUNCHES IN FEBRUARY (on sale in early January) WITH THREE BREATHTAKING NOVELS . . .**

### THE WIND DANCER
*by Iris Johansen*

### TEXAS! LUCKY
*by Sandra Brown*

### WAITING WIVES
*by Christina Harland*

## THE WIND DANCER.

From the spellbinding pen of Iris Johansen comes her most lush, dramatic, and emotionally touching romance yet—a magnificent historical about characters whose lives have been touched by the legendary Wind Dancer. A glorious antiquity, the Wind Dancer is a statue of a Pegasus that is encrusted with jewels . . . but whose worth is beyond the value of its precious stones, gold, and artistry. The Wind Dancer's origins are shrouded in the mist of time . . . and only a chosen few can unleash its mysterious powers. But WIND DANCER is, first and foremost, a magnificent love story. Set in Renaissance Italy where intrigues were as intricate as carved cathedral doors and affairs of state were ruled by affairs of the bedchamber. WIND DANCER tells the captivating story of the lovely and indomitable slave Sanchia and the man who bought her on a back street in Florence. Passionate, powerful *condottiere* Lionello Andreas would love Sanchia and endanger her with equal wild abandon as he sought to win back the prized possession of his family, the Wind Dancer.

## TEXAS! LUCKY.

Turning her formidable talent for the first time to the creation of a trilogy, Sandra Brown gives readers a family to remember in the Tylers—brothers Lucky and Chase and their "little" sister Sage. In oil-bust country where Texas millionaires are becoming Texas panhandlers, the Tylers are struggling to keep their drilling business from bankruptcy. Each of the TEXAS! novels tells the love story of one member of the family and combines gritty and colorful characters with the fluid and sensual style the author is lauded for!

## WAITING WIVES.

By marvelously talented newcomer Christina Harland, WAITING WIVES is the riveting tale of three vastly different women from different countries whose only bond is the fate of their men who are missing in Vietnam. In this unique novel of great human emotion, full of danger, bravery, and romance, Christina Harland brings to the written page what CHINA BEACH and TOUR OF DUTY have brought to television screens. This is a novel of triumph and honor and hope . . . and love.

Rave reviews are pouring in from critics and much-loved authors on FANFARE's novels for February—and for those in months to come. You'll be delighted and enthralled by works by Amanda Quick and Beverly Byrne, Roseanne Bittner and Kay Hooper, Susan Johnson and Nora Roberts . . . to mention only a few of the remarkable authors in the FAN-FARE imprint.

Special authors. Special covers. And very special stories.

Can you hear the flourish of trumpets now . . . the flourish of trumpets announcing that something special is coming?

# FANFARE

*Brief excerpts of the launch novels along with praise for them is on the following pages.*

New York *Times* bestselling authors Catherine Coulter and Julie Garwood praise the advance copy they read of **WIND DANCER:**

> "Iris Johansen is a bestselling author for the best of reasons—she's a wonderful storyteller. Sanchia, Lion, Lorenzo, and Caterina will wrap themselves around your heart and move right in. Enjoy, I did!"
> —Catherine Coulter

> "So compelling, so unforgettable a page-turner, this enthralling tale could have been written only by Iris Johansen. I never wanted to leave the world she created with Sanchia and Lion at its center."
> —Julie Garwood

In the following brief excerpt you'll see why *Romantic Times* said this about Iris Johansen and **THE WIND DANCER:**

> "The formidable talent of Iris Johansen blazes into incandescent brilliance in this highly original, mesmerizing love story."

We join the story as the evil Carpino, who runs a ring of prostitutes and thieves in Florence, is forcing the young heroine Sanchia to "audition" as a thief for the great *condottiere* Lionello, who waits in the piazza with his friend, Lorenzo, observing at a short distance.

"You're late!" Caprino jerked Sanchia into the shadows of the arcade surrounding the piazza.

"It couldn't be helped," Sanchia said breathlessly. "There was an accident . . . and we didn't get finished until the hour tolled . . . and then I had to wait until Giovanni left to take the—"

Caprino silenced the flow of words with an impatient motion of his hand. "There he is." He nodded across the crowded piazza. "The big man in the wine-colored velvet cape listening to the storyteller."

Sanchia's gaze followed Caprino's to the man standing in front of the platform. He was more than big, he was a giant, she thought gloomily. The careless arrogance in the man's stance bespoke perfect confidence in his ability to deal with any circumstances and, if he caught her, he'd probably use his big strong hands to crush her head like a walnut. Well, she was too tired to worry about that now. It had been over thirty hours since she had slept. Perhaps it was just as well she was almost too exhausted to care what happened to her. Fear must not make her as clumsy as she had been yesterday. She was at least glad the giant appeared able to afford to lose a few ducats. The richness of his clothing indicated he must either be a great lord or a prosperous merchant.

"Go." Caprino gave her a little push out onto the piazza. "Now."

She pulled her shawl over her head to shadow her face and hurried toward the platform where a man was telling a story, accompanying himself on the lyre.

A drop of rain struck her face, and she glanced up at the suddenly dark skies. Not yet, she thought with exasperation. If it started to rain in earnest the people crowding the piazza would run for shelter and she would have to follow the velvet-clad giant until he put himself into a situation that allowed her to make the snatch.

Another drop splashed her hand, and her anxious gaze flew to the giant. His attention was still fixed on the storyteller, but only the saints knew how long he would remain engrossed. This storyteller was not very good. Her pace quickened as she flowed like a shadow into the crowd surrounding the platform.

Garlic, Lion thought, as the odor assaulted his nostrils. Garlic, spoiled fish, and some other stench that smelled even fouler. He glanced around the crowd trying to identify the source of the smell. The people surrounding the platform were the same ones he had studied moments before, trying to search out Caprino's thief. The only new arrival was a thin woman dressed in a shabby gray gown, an equally ragged woolen shawl covering her head.

She moved away from the edge of the crowd and started to hurry across the piazza. The stench faded with her departure and Lion drew a deep breath. *Dio*, luck was with him in this, at least. He was not at all pleased at being forced to stand in the rain waiting for Caprino to produce his master thief.

"It's done," Lorenzo muttered, suddenly at Lion's side. He had been watching from the far side of the crowd. Now he said more loudly, "As sweet a snatch as I've ever seen."

"What?" Frowning, Lion gazed at him. "There was no—" He broke off as he glanced down at his belt. The pouch was gone; only the severed cords remained in his belt. "Sweet Jesus." His gaze flew around the piazza. "Who?"

"The sweet madonna who looked like a beggar maid and smelled like a decaying corpse." Lorenzo nodded toward the arched arcade. "She disappeared behind that column, and I'll wager you'll find Caprino lurking there with her, counting your ducats."

Lion started toward the column. "A woman," he murmured. "I didn't expect a woman. How good is she?"

Lorenzo fell into step with him. "Very good."

Iris Johansen's fabulous romances of characters whose lives are touched by the Wind Dancer go on! STORM WINDS, coming from FANFARE in June 1991, is another historical. REAP THE WIND, a contemporary, will be published by FANFARE in November 1991.

Sandra Brown, whose legion of fans catapulted her last contemporary novel onto the *New York Times* list, has received the highest praise in advance reviews of **TEXAS! LUCKY.** *Rave Reviews* said, "Romance fans will relish all of Ms. Brown's provocative sensuality along with a fast-paced plotline that springs one surprise after another. Another feast for the senses from one of the world's hottest pens."

Indeed Sandra's pen is "hot"—especially so in her incredible **TEXAS!** trilogy. We're going to peek in on an early episode in which Lucky has been hurt in a brawl in a bar where he was warding off the attentions of two town bullies toward a redhead he hadn't met, but wanted to get to know very well.

This woman was going to be an exciting challenge, something rare that didn't come along every day. Hell, he'd never had anybody exactly like her.

"What's your name?"

She raised deep forest-green eyes to his. "D-D Dovey."

" 'D-D Dovey'?"

"That's right," she snapped defensively. "What's wrong with it?"

"Nothing. I just hadn't noticed your stuttering before. Or has the sight of my bare chest made you develop a speech impediment?"

"Hardly. Mr.—?"

"Lucky."

"Mr. Lucky?"

"No, I'm Lucky."

"Why is that?"

"I mean my name is Lucky. Lucky Tyler."

"Oh. Well. I assure you the sight of your bare chest leaves me cold, Mr. Tyler."

He didn't believe her and the smile that tilted up one corner of his mouth said so. "Call me Lucky."

She reached for the bottle of whiskey on the nightstand and raised it in salute. "Well, Lucky, your luck just ran out."

"Huh?"

"Hold your breath." Before he could draw a sufficient one, she tipped the bottle and drizzled the liquor over the cut.

He blasted the four walls with words unfit to be spoken aloud, much less shouted. "Oh hell, oh—"

"Your language isn't becoming to a gentleman, Mr. Tyler."

"I'm gonna murder you. Stop pouring that stuff— Agh!"

"You're acting like a big baby."

"What the hell are you trying to do, scald me?"

"Kill the germs."

"Damn! It's killing *me*. Do something. Blow on it."

"That only causes germs to spread."

"Blow on it!"

She bent her head over his middle and blew gently along the cut. Her breath fanned his skin and cooled the stinging whiskey in the open wound. Droplets of it had collected in the satiny stripe of hair beneath his navel. Rivulets trickled beneath the waistband of his jeans. She blotted at them with her fingertips, then, without thinking, licked the liquor off her own skin. When she realized what she'd done, she sprang upright. "Better now?" she asked huskily.

When Lucky's blue eyes connected with hers, it was like completing an electric circuit. The atmosphere crackled. Matching her husky tone of voice, he said, "Yeah, much better. . . . Thanks," he mumbled. Her hand felt so comforting and cool, the way his mother's always had whenever he was sick with fever. He captured Dovey's hand with his and pressed it against his hot cheek.

She withdrew it and, in a schoolmarm's voice, said, "You can stay only until the swelling goes down."

"I don't think I'll be going anywhere a-tall tonight," he said. "I feel like hell. This is all I want to do. Lie here. Real still and quiet."

Through a mist of pain, he watched her remove her jacket and drape it over the back of a chair. Just as he'd thought—quite a looker was Dovey. But that wasn't all. She looked like a woman who knew her own mind and wasn't afraid to speak it. Levelheaded.

So what the hell had she been doing in that bar? He drifted off while puzzling through the question.

Now on sale in DOUBLEDAY hardcover is the next in Sandra's fantastic trilogy, TEXAS! CHASE, about which *Rendezvous* has said: ". . . it's the story of a love that is deeper than the oceans, and more lasting than the land itself. Lucky's story was fantastic; Chase's story is more so." FANFARE's paperback of TEXAS! CHASE will go on sale August 1991.

Rather than excerpt from the extraordinary novel **WAITING WIVES**, which focuses on three magnificent women, we will describe the book in some detail. The three heroines whom you'll love and root for give added definition to the words growth and courage . . . and love.

**ABBRA** is talented and sheltered, a raven-haired beauty who was just eighteen when she fell rapturously in love with handsome Army captain Lewis Ellis. Immediately after their marriage he leaves for Vietnam. Passionately devoted to Lewis, she lives for his return—until she's told he's dead. Then her despair turns to torment as she falls hopelessly in love with Lewis's irresistible brother. . . .

**SERENA** never regrets her wildly impulsive marriage to seductive Kyle Anderson. But she does regret her life of unabashed decadence and uninhibited pleasure—especially when she discovers a dirty, bug-infested orphanage in Saigon . . . and Kyle's illegitimate child.

**GABRIELLE** is the daughter of a French father and a Vietnamese mother. A flame-haired singer with urchin appeal and a sultry voice, she is destined for stardom. But she gives her heart—and a great part of her future—to a handsome Aussie war correspondent. Gavin is determined to record the "real" events of the Vietnam war . . . but his search for truth leads him straight into the hands of the Viet Cong and North Vietnamese, who have no intention of letting him report anything until they've won the war.

Christina Harland is an author we believe in. Her story is one that made all of us who work on FANFARE cry, laugh, and turn pages like mad. We predict that WAITING WIVES will fascinate and enthrall you . . . and that you will say with us, "it is a novel whose time has come."

We hope you will greet FANFARE next month with jubilation! It is an imprint we believe you will delight in month after month, year after year to come.

# THE "VIVE LA ROMANCE" SWEEPSTAKES

## Don't miss your chance to speak to your favorite Loveswept authors on the LOVESWEPT LINE  1-900-896-2505*

You may win a glorious week for two in the world's most romantic city, Paris, France by entering the "Vive La Romance" sweepstakes when you call. With travel arrangements made by Reliable Travel, you and that special someone will fly American Airlines to Paris, where you'll be guests at the famous Lancaster Hotel. Why not call right now? Your own Loveswept fantasy could come true!

### Official Rules:

1. **No Purchase Is Necessary**. Enter by calling 1-900-896-2505 and following the directions for entry. The phone call will cost $.95 per minute and the average time necessary to enter the sweepstakes will be two minutes or less with either a touch tone or a rotary phone, when you choose to enter at the beginning of the call. Or you can enter by handprinting your name, address and telephone number on a plain 3" x 5" card and sending it to:

> **VIVE LA ROMANCE SWEEPSTAKES**
> **Department CK**
> **BANTAM BOOKS**
> **666 Fifth Avenue**
> **New York, New York 10103**

Copies of the Official Rules can be obtained by sending a request along with a self-addressed stamped envelope to: Vive La Romance Sweepstakes, Bantam Books, Department CK-2, 666 Fifth Avenue, New York, New York 10103. Residents of Washington and Vermont need not include return postage. Requests must be received by November 30, 1990.

*Callers must be 18 or older. Each call costs 95¢ per minute. See official rules for details.

Official Rules cont'd

2. 1 Grand Prize: A vacation trip for two to Paris, France for 7 nights.Trip includes accommodations at the deluxe Lancaster Hotel and round-trip coach tickets to Paris on American Airlines from the American Airlines airport nearest the winner's residence which provides direct service to New York.
(Approximate Retail Value: $3,500).

3. Sweepstakes begins October 1, 1990 and all entries must be received by December 31, 1990. All entrants must be 18 years of age or older at the time of entry. The winner will be chosen by Bantam's Marketing Department by a random drawing to be held on or about January 15, 1991 from all entries received and will be notified by mail. Bantam's decision is final. The winner has 30 days from date of notice in which to accept the prize award or an alternate winner will be chosen. The prize is not transferable and no substitution is allowed. The trip must be taken by November 22, 1991, and is subject to airline departure schedules and ticket and accommodation availability. Certain blackout periods may apply. Winner must have a valid passport. Odds of winning depend on the number of entries received. Enter as often as you wish, but each mail-in entry must be entered separately. No mechanically reproduced entries allowed.

4. The winner and his or her guest will be required to execute an Affidavit of Eligibility and Promotional Release supplied by Bantam. Entering the sweepstakes constitutes permission for use of winner's name, address and likeness for publicity and promotional purposes, with no additional compensation or permission.

5. This sweepstakes is open only to residents of the U.S. who are 18 years of age or older, and is void in Puerto Rico and wherever else prohibited or restricted by law. Employees of Bantam Books, Bantam Doubleday Dell Publishing Group, Inc., Reliable Travel, Call Interactive, their subsidiaries and affiliates, and their immediate family members are not eligible to enter this sweepstakes. Taxes, if any, are the winner's sole responsibility.

6. Bantam is the sole sponsor of the sweepstakes. Bantam reserves the right to cancel the sweepstakes via the 900 number at any time and without prior notice, but entry into the sweepstakes via mail through December 31, 1990 will remain. Bantam is not responsible for lost, delayed or misdirected entries, and Bantam, Call Interactive, and AT&T are not responsible for any error, incorrect or inaccurate entry of information by entrants, malfunctions of the telephone network, computer equipment software or any combination thereof. This Sweepstakes is subject to the complete Official Rules.

7. For the name of the prize winner (available after January 15, 1991), send a stamped, self-addressed envelope entirely separate from your entry to:

VIVE LA ROMANCE SWEEPSTAKES WINNER LIST,
Bantam Books, Dept. CK-3, 666 Fifth Avenue,
New York, New York 10103.

*Loveswept* ®